# GHOSTLY ENCOUNTERS

*Ghostly Encounters* is a companion volume to the Lion, *Ghostly Experiences*. Published originally as part of the hardback collection entitled *The Restless Ghost*, *Ghostly Encounters* offers such spine-chilling authors as Leon Garfield, W. F. Harvey, L. P. Hartley, William Croft Dickinson and W. W. Jacobs.

Would you care to meet a mason cutting *your* tombstone, with the date of death already on it? Read *August Heat*. Or *The Monkey's Paw* with its power to grant three wishes—which nobody *ever* wanted. These, and more ghostly encounters to make the hair rise on the back of your neck!

'A splendid collection of supernatural adventures.'
*New Statesman*

'The stories in this collection have been chosen with discrimination and illustrated with a sure intuition.'
*Growing Point*

# GHOSTLY ENCOUNTERS

Chosen by
SUSAN DICKINSON

Illustrated by
Anthony Maitland

COLLINS: LIONS

First published 1970
as part of the collection, *The Restless Ghost*
by William Collins Sons and Co Ltd
14 St James's Place, London SW1
First published in Lions 1973

Printed in Great Britain
by William Collins Sons and Co Ltd, Glasgow

# CONTENTS

# ACKNOWLEDGMENTS

The Editor and Publishers are grateful to the following for permission to reprint copyright material in this anthology:

Winant Towers Ltd for *The Restless Ghost* © 1969 by Leon Garfield;

Hamish Hamilton Ltd for *Feet Foremost* from *The Collected Stories of L. P. Hartley* © 1968 L. P. Hartley (Hamish Hamilton, London);

J. M. Dent & Sons Ltd for *August Heat* from *The Beast With Five Fingers* by W. F. Harvey;

The Executors of William Croft Dickinson for *The Return of The Native* from *Dark Encounters* published by the Harvill Press © 1963 William Croft Dickinson;

Charles Lavell Ltd for *Coincidence* from *The Best of A. J. Alan* © 1962 by A. J. Alan;

Edward Arnold (Publishers) Ltd. for *The Rose Garden* from *Collected Ghost Stories* by M. R. James;

The Society of Authors as the literary representative of the Estate of W. W. Jacobs for *The Monkey's Paw*;

The author for *Ghost Riders of the Sioux* © 1970 by Kenneth Ulyatt.

# The Restless Ghost

LEON GARFIELD

D'you know the old church at Hove – the ruined one that lies three-quarters of a mile back from the sea and lets the moon through like a church of black Nottingham lace?

Not an agreeable place, with its tumbledown churchyard brooded over by twelve elms and four threadbare yews which seemed to be in mourning for better weather. A real disgrace to the Christian dead.

Twice a month the vicar used to preach briefly; then be glad to get back to Preston. For he, no more than anyone, liked the villainous old crow of a sexton.

A mean, shrivelled, horny, sour, fist-shaking and shouting old man was the sexton, a hater of most things, but particularly boys.

Some said the reason for his ill-temper was a grumbling belly; others said it was bunions (on account of his queer bounding limp when chasing off marauders and young hooters among his tombs); and others muttered that he was plagued by a ghost.

D'you remember the ghost? It was a drummer boy who used to drift through the churchyard on misty Saturday nights, glowing blue and green and drumming softly – to the unspeakable terror of all.

But that was twenty years ago. Then, two years after the haunting had begun, a certain band of smugglers had been caught and hanged – every last one of them in a dismal, dancing line – but not before they'd made a weird confession. They said the ghostly drummer had been no worse than a foundling lad, smeared with phosphorus to glow and gleam and scare off interruption while the smugglers followed darkly on. For the churchyard had been their secret pathway to the safety of the Downs and beyond.

But that was eighteen years ago. The foundling lad had vanished and the smugglers had all mouldered away. So why was the old sexton such a misery and so violent against idly mischievous boys? What had they ever done to him (save hoot and squeak among his graves), so that he should rush out and threaten them with his spade and an old musket that was no more use than a rotten branch?

An interesting question; and one that absorbed two pupils of Dr Barron's school in Brighthelmstone to the exclusion of their proper studies. Their names? Dick Bostock and his dear friend, R. Harris.

'What say we scare the dying daylights out of him on Saturday night?' said Bostock to Harris on the Wednesday before it.

Harris, who was a physician's son and therefore interested in all things natural and supernatural, nodded his large head. Harris was thirteen and somewhat the more intellectual; but Bostock, though younger by a year, was the more widely profound. Even separately, they were of consequence, but together they were of sombre ingenuity and frantic daring.

So it was that, during three long and twilight walks to their separate homes, they hit on a singularly eerie scheme.

And all the while, in his cottage by the lych-gate, brooded the savage old sexton, unknowing that his angry days were numbered; and that two formidable pupils of Dr Barron's had cast up their score.

'I'll give him something to moan about!' said Bostock, deeply.

'That you will,' agreed Harris, with a gloomy admiration . . . for his part in the strange scheme was limited to fetching its wherewithal.

They met for the final time on the Saturday afternoon – as the light was dying – in an obscure lane two
hundred yards to the north of the church.

They met in silence, as became their enterprise; but
with nods and smiles, as became the success of it.

They walked for a little way till they came to a
break in the hedge that led to a spot of some secrecy.
There they unburdened themselves of their bundles.

'On a misty Saturday night . . .' murmured Bostock,
drawing out of his bundle a scarlet and black striped
coat.

'. . . There walked among the graves,' whispered Harris, producing an old grenadier's cap.

'A fearful, ghostly drummer boy,' said Bostock, bringing forth the necessary drum that rattled softly as he
laid it in the long, stiff grass. He paused, then added:

'Glowing?'

'Blue and green,' nodded Harris, holding up a small
stone pot, stolen from his father's laboratory.

In this was the phosphorescent paint – an eerie mix-
ture of yellow phosphates and pigmented ointment –
furtively compounded by Harris from the recipe he had
copied out of the condemned smuggler's confession.

The clothes they had borrowed off a brandy mer-
chant whose son had gone for a soldier and not come
back – were exactly as the smugglers had declared.
('We dressed him as a grenadier, yer Honour. 'Twas all
we had to hand.')

Hurriedly – for the day was almost gone – Dick Bostock put the garments on. As he did so, he felt a strange,
martial urge quicken his heart and run through his
veins.

He took the drum, slung it about his neck – and
could scarcely prevent himself from rolling and rattling
upon it then and there.

Instead of which, watched by the silent Harris, he marched stiffly up and down as if possessed by the spirits of all the valorous youths who'd ever gone to war. Indeed, so brightly gleamed his eyes, that he might well have done without the ghostly paint; but Harris, whose masterpiece it was, now offered it with a trembling hand.

'Now the sea mist's come, it'll not be dangerous,' he murmured, shivering slightly as a heavy damp came drifting through the hedge.

'Dangerous?' said Bostock scornfully.

'Moistness is necessary,' said Harris, stroking the pot. 'It takes fire or burns in dry air. But the mists will keep it damp . . .' Then, clutched with a sudden uneasiness, he muttered urgently: 'Bostock! don't be overlong.'

'Come Harris! Open it up! Paint me, Harris. Make me glow and gleam. I'll be but half an hour in the churchyard. More than enough to frighten that dismal pig out of his wits. Then I'll be back with you safe and sound. I'll not outstay the mists – I promise you! Don't shake and shiver, Harris! D'you think I aim to stand among the tombs till I take fire and frizzle like a sausage?'

Harris continued to shiver; but even so, his more cautious soul was shamed before Bostock's valour . . . which appeared even more striking by reason of the grenadier's cap and drum.

He opened the pot. And from it, as if there had been something within that had been sleeping – a monstrous glow-worm, maybe – there came slowly forth a pale, evil gleaming . . .

Little by little, this uncanny light increased, shedding its queer radiance on the boys' peering faces – and beyond them to the dense hawthorns that clustered about, touching the tips of the twigs with the bright buds of a Devil's Spring.

'Paint me, Harris,' breathed Bostock.

So Harris, with a spatula stolen from his father's dispensary, began to smear the weird ointment on to the drummer's coat, his cuffs, his grenadier's cap, the front of his breeches, the tarnished cords of his drum, the drumsticks, and –

'My face, Harris. Dab some on my face!'

'No, not there, Bostock! Not your face! There may be danger from it . . .'

'Then my hands, Harris. You must paint my hands!'

Once more, Harris was overcome. With the spatula that shook so much that the evil substance spattered the grass with its chilly gleaming, he scraped a thin layer on the young skin of Bostock's hands.

To Bostock the ointment felt unnaturally cold – even piercingly so. The heavy chill of it seemed to sink into the bones of his fingers and from thence to creep upward . . .

With a scowl of contempt at his own imagining, he seized up the shining drumsticks – and brought them down on the drum with a sharp and formidable sound. Then again . . . and again, till the sticks quivered on the stretched skin as if in memory of the ominous rattle of war. And he began to stalk to and fro . . .

Harris fell back, transfixed with a terrified admiration. Glowing green and blue, with bony rattle and a shadowy smile, there marched the ghostly drummer to the very mockery of life.

'Am I fearful?' whispered Bostock, stopping the drumming and overcome with awe at the terror in his companion's eyes.

'Horrible, Bostock. Did I not know it was you, I'd drop down stone dead with fright.'

'Do I walk like a ghost?' pursued Bostock.

Harris, who'd never viewed a ghost, considered it would need a pretty remarkable spectre to come even within moaning distance of the grim and ghastly Bostock. He nodded.

'Then let's be gone,' said Bostock, as hollowly as he might. 'Watch from a distance, Harris. See without being seen.'

Again, Harris nodded. Whereupon the phosphorescent drummer stalked eerily off, drumming as he went, towards the silent church.

The sea mists were now visiting among the elms of the churchyard, sometimes drifting out like bulky grey widows, for to peer at the inscription on some tumbled altar-tomb, before billowing off as in search of another, dearer one . . .

The light from the sexton's cottage glimmered fitfully among the branches of one of the yews – for all the world as if the angry old man had at last given up human company and made his home in that dark, tangled place.

Bostock, watched by fascinated Harris from the churchyard's edge – smiled deeply, and stalked on.

Drum . . . drum . . . drum! the battalions are coming! From where? From the mists and the shuddering tombs . . . platoons of long dead grenadiers pricked up their bony heads at the call of the old drum; grinned – nodded – moved to arms . . .

Or so it seemed to the phosphorescent Bostock as he trundled back and forth, uneasily enjoying himself and awaiting the sexton's terror.

Now the sound of his drum seemed to echo – doubtless by reason of the confining mists. He must remember to ask Harris about it. Harris knew of such things. (Also the banking vapours seemed to reflect back, here and there, his own phosphorescence, as if in a foul mirror.)

Sea mists were queer; especially at night. But he was grateful that their heavy damp eased the tingling on his hands. The ointment was indeed a powerful one.

There was no sign yet of the sexton. Was it possible he hadn't heard the drum? Could the horrible old man have gone deaf? With a touch of irritation, Bostock began to drum more loudly, and stalked among the tombs that lay closest to the cottage.

He hoped the mists and elms had not quite swallowed him up from Harris's view. After all, he'd no wish to perform for the night and the dead alone (supposing the sexton never came). Harris ought to get some benefit. Besides which, a most gloomy loneliness was come upon him. A melancholy loneliness, the like of which he'd never known.

'Harris!' he called softly; but was too far off to be heard by the physician's son.

Suddenly, he must have passed into a curious nestling of mists. The echo of his drum seemed to have become more distinct. Strange effect of nature. Harris would be interested.

'Harris . . .'

There seemed to be layers in the mist . . . first soft and tumbled, then smooth.

These smooth patches, he fancied he glimpsed through shifting holes. Or believed he did. For once more he seemed to be reflected in them – then lost from sight – then back again . . . glowing briefly blue and green.

'Harris . . .'

Now the reflected image stayed longer. Marched with him . . . drummed with him . . .

Yet in that mirror made of mist, there was a strange

deception. No ointment had been applied to Bostock's
face, yet this shadow drummer's narrow brow and
sunken cheeks were glowing with —

'Harris!'

But Harris never heard him. Harris had fled. Harris,
from his watching place beyond the graves, had observed that his gleaming friend had attracted a companion. Another, palely glowing grenadier!

'Harris — Harris — ' moaned the painted Bostock as the
terrible drummer paused and stared at him with eyes
that were no eyes but patches of blackness in a tragic,
mouldered face.

Suddenly, the terrified boy recovered the use of his
legs; or, rather, his legs recovered the use of the boy.
And wrenched him violently away.

In truth, he did not know he'd begun to run, till

running he'd been for seconds. Like a wounded firefly, he twittered and stumbled and wove wildly among the graves. All his frantic daring was now abruptly changed into its reverse. Frantic terror engulfed him – and was doubled each time he looked back.

And the phantom drummer was following . . . drumming as it came . . . staring as if with reproach for the living boy's mockery of its unhappy state.

Now out of the churchyard fled the boy, much hampered by his ridiculous costume and overlarge drum, which thumped as his knees struck it – like a huge, hollow heart.

Into the lane whence he'd come, he rushed. He might have been a craven soldier, flying some scene of battle, with his spectral conscience in pursuit.

At the end of the lane, he paused; groaned 'Harris!' miserably once more; but no Harris answered; only the drum . . . drum . . . drum! of the phantom he'd drawn in his wake.

Very striking was its aspect now, as it drifted out of the shadows of the lane. Its clothing was threadbare – and worse. Its cap was on the large size . . . as were the cuffs that hung upon the ends of its bone-thin fingers like strange, frayed mouths.

And on its face was a look of glaring sadness, most sombre to behold.

Not that Bostock was much inclined to behold it, or to make its closer acquaintance in any way.

Yet even though he'd turned and fled, trembling on, the tragic drummer's face remained printed on his inward eye . . .

'I'm going home – going home!' sobbed Bostock as he ran. 'You can't come with me there!'

But the sound of the drum grew no fainter . . . and the spectre followed on.

'What do you want with me? What have I done?

I'm Dick Bostock – and nought to you! Dick Bostock, d'you hear? A stranger – no more!'

Drum . . . drum . . . drum! came on behind him; and, when the boy helplessly turned, he saw on the phantom's face a look of unearthly hope!

'This is my home!' sobbed the boy at last, when he came to the comfortable little road he knew so well. 'Leave me now!'

He stumbled down the row of stout flint cottages till he came to his own. With shaking fingers, he un-latched his garden gate.

'Leave me! Leave me!'

Drum . . . drum . . . drum! came relentless down the street.

'Now I'm safe – now I'm safe!' moaned Bostock, for he'd come to the back of his house.

There, under the roof, was his bedroom window, in which a candle warmly burned.

Of a sudden: the terrible drumming stopped. 'Thank God!' whispered Bostock.

He drew in his breath, prayed – and looked behind him.

'Thank God!' he whispered again: the phantom was gone.

Now he turned to his home and hastened to climb up an old apple tree that had ever served him for stairs. He reached the longed-for window. He looked within. He gave a groan of terror and dismay.

In his room, seated on his bed, looking out of his window – was the horrible drummer again.

And, as the living boy stared palely in, so the dead one stared out . . . then, it lifted up its arm and pointed.

It pointed unmistakably past the unhappy Bostock . . . over his shoulder and towards the churchyard whence it had come.

There was no doubt of its meaning. None at all. Bostock must fill the place left vacant in the church-yard. His own had just been taken.

Never was a live boy worse situated. Never had an apple tree borne whiter fruit . . . that now dropped down, dismally phosphorescent, to the cold, damp ground.

The miserable Bostock, phosphorescent as ever, stood forlornly under the apple tree. The phantom had caught him and trapped him most malevolently.

To appear as he was, at his own front door, was more than his courage or compassion allowed.

His father and mother's fury on his awesome appear-ance, he could have endured. But there was worse than that. Would they not have died of fright when they faced his usurper – the grim inhabitant of his room – that other shining drummer boy?

Tears of misery and despair stood in his eyes, ran over and fell upon his tingling hands.

Harris! He must go to Harris, the physician's large-headed son. Wise old Harris . . .

He crept out into the road and ran deviously to a prosperous house that stood on the corner. Candles were shining in the parlour window and the good doc-tor and his lady were sat on either side of their fire. But Harris was not with them. Bostock flitted to the back of the house. Harris's bedroom was aglow. He had returned.

'Harris!' called Bostock, urgently. But Harris's win-dow was tight shut, against the damp air . . . and more.

'Harris! For pity's sake, Harris!'

No answer. Harris had heard nothing save, most likely, the uneasy pounding of his own heart.

Desperately, Bostock cast about for pebbles to fling at the window. With no success. What then? The drum! He would tap on the drum. Harris would hear that. For certain sure, Harris would hear that.

And Harris did hear it. Came to his window aghast. Ever of a studious, pimplish disposition; his spots burned now like little fiery mountains in the ashes of his face. Not knowing which drummer he was beholding, he took it for the worse. Bostock would have shouted; Bostock would have thrown pebbles at the window . . . not beaten the evil drum!

He vanished from his window with a soundless cry of dismay. His curtain was drawn rapidly and Bostock — faintly shining Bostock — was left, rejected of the living.

So he began to walk, choosing the loneliest, darkest ways. Twice he frightened murmuring lovers, winding softly home. But he got no pleasure from it . . .

Glumly, he wondered if this was a sign of slipping into true ghostliness.

This mournful thought led to another, even sadder. He wondered if the phantom in his bedroom was now losing its weird glow, and generally filling out into a perfect likeness of the boy whose place it had stolen.

Very likely. Nature and un-nature, so to speak, were disagreeably tidy. They cared for nothing left over. Vague and confused memories of Dr Barron's classroom, sleep-provoking voice filled his head . . . and he wished he'd attended more carefully. He felt the lack of solid learning in which he might have found an answer to his plight.

Ghosts, phantoms, unquiet spirits of all denominations stalked the earth for a purpose. And until that purpose was achieved, they were doomed to continue in their melancholy office.

This much, Bostock had a grasp of: but if ever Dr Barron had let fall anything further that might have been of help, Bostock could not remember it. Neither tag nor notion nor fleeting word remained in his head. He was alone and shining – and his hands were beginning to burn.

Of a sudden, he found himself in the lane that wound to the north of the church. Back to the churchyard he was being driven, by forces outside his reckoning.

'Good-bye, Harris,' he whispered, as he stumbled through the broken hedge and across the grass towards the night-pierced bulk of the ruined church. 'Good-bye for ever.'

The thick grass muttered against his legs and his drum grumbled softly under his lifting knees.

'Good-bye, light of day; good-bye Dr Barron; good-bye my mother and father; good-bye my friends and enemies; good-bye my cat Jupiter and my dear mice . . . Oh Harris, Harris! Remember me! Remember your young friend Bostock – who went for a ghost and never came back!'

And then, with a pang of bitterness the thought returned that the spectre would have become another Bostock. Harris would have no cause to remember what Harris would never know had gone.

When he found himself among the elms the anger vanished. Instead Bostock sadly, resignedly surveyed his future realm.

There lay the graves, all leaning and tumbled like stone ships, frozen in a stormy black sea. The mists were almost gone and the starlight glimmered coldly down. What was he to do? How best discharge his new office? The drum, that was it, beat the drum and drift uncannily to and fro.

So he began, drum . . . drum . . . drum! But, it must be admitted, he tended to stumble rather than to drift; for, where a phantom might have floated, Bostock trod. Many a time he caught his bruised feet in roots that were more uncanny than he. But there was yet something more frightening than that. His hands were burning more and more.

He tried to subdue the pain by thinking on other things. But what thoughts could come to a boy in a dark churchyard save unwelcome ones?

He gave several dismal groans, even more pitiful than a wandering spirit might have uttered. His poor hands were afire . . .

Water – he must have water! He felt in the long grass for such damp as the mists might have left behind. Too little . . . too little. He ran from grave to grave, laying his hands against the cold, moist stone. To no purpose. He looked to the ragged, broken church . . . Of a sudden, a hope plucked at his heart.

There was to be a christening on the morrow. A fisherman's child . . . Already, it had been delayed for two months on account of a chill. Harris – interested in all such matters – had sagely talked of it. ('In my opinion, they ought to wait another month. But there's no arguing with superstitious fisherfolk! They'll douse the brat on Sunday, come snivel, come sneeze, come galloping decline!')

The font! Maybe it was already filled?

Bostock began to run. A frantic sight, his luminous knees thumped the underside of the drum setting up the rapid thunder of an advance. His luminous sleeves, his gleaming cuffs with his distracted hands held high, flared through the night like shining banners. And, as he passed them by, the old cracked tombstones seemed to gape in amazement – and lean as if to follow.

At last, he reached the church; halted, briefly prayed, and crept inside.

All was gloom and deep shadows, and the night wind blowing through rents in the stone caused the empty pews to creak and sigh as if under the memory of generations of Sunday sleepers . . .

Bostock approached the font. Thank God for Christian fisherfolk! It was filled.

With huge relief, he sank his wretched, shining hands into the icy water. They glimmered against the stone beneath the water like nightmarish fish ... But oh! the blessed stoppage of the pain!

He stood, staring towards the altar, upon which, from a higher hole in the roof, such light as was in the night sky dropped gently down.

He started; and, in so doing, scraped the drum against the font. It rattled softly through the dark.

What had made him to start? He was not alone in the church. A figure was crouched upon the altar step. A figure seemingly sunk in sleep or prayer or stony brooding ...

On the sound of the drum, the figure turned – and groaned to its feet.

It was the sour and savage old sexton. Bitter moment for Bostock. Too late now to get any joy out of frightening the old man stupid. Bostock, his hands in the font, was more frightened by far. Unhappily, he awaited the old man's wrath.

But the old man only stood and stared at him. There was no rage in his withered face; only wonderment and fear. Nor was it a sudden fear, such as a man might betray on first seeing a ghost. It was the deep, abiding fear of a man to whom a ghost came often – to plague him on misty Saturday nights. For in the shadow of the church, he took the glimmering Bostock to be that phantom that had troubled him this many a long year. Yet ... with a difference –

'Into the church?' he whispered. 'Even into the church, now? What does it mean? You never came in the church before. Is it – is it forgiveness, at last?'

Bostock stared at the shrivelled old sexton – that terror of marauding boys. Very miserable and desolate was the ancient wretch. Very pitiful was the hope in his eyes –

'Yes!' cried the sexton, with misguided joy. 'It's forgiveness! I see it in your eyes! Pity! Blessed, blessed pity!'

Fearful to speak, or even to move, Bostock gazed at the old man who now hobbled towards him. There was a look of tarnished radiance on his face as secrets long knotted in his heart began to unravel and give him peace.

'At last my treasure, dear spirit! Now I can go to it! It's all right now? In this holy place, you've come to forgive? My treasure! All these years of waiting for it! All these years of misery . . . all these years of longing . . . How many? Eighteen! But all's forgiven now . . . at last, at last!'

Careless of the raging ointment, Bostock drew his hands out of the font as the old man tottered by, mumbling and gabbling as he went.

For the old man did pass him by, his face quite transfigured by yearning and relief. He went out into the tumbledown churchyard, clucking over the neglected graves like an ancient gardener, revisiting an overgrown garden he'd once tended well . . .

Absorbed beyond measure, the luminous Bostock followed – straining to catch the drift of the old man's broken words.

There was no doubt now, the ghost had been that of the foundling boy who'd long ago drummed for the smugglers. Likewise, there was no doubt that the sexton had brought him to his death.

'I never knew you was ailing, my dear. I never knew the paint was a-poisoning you. I swear I'd never have made you go out when the mists was gone if I'd known! Ask the others – if you're situated to do so. They'll tell you I never knew. Thought you was pretending for more of the haul. Thought your cries and moans were play-acting. Never, never thought you'd die, my dear!'

Thus he mumbled and muttered – half over his shoulder – to what he fancied was the ghost he hoped had forgiven him at last.

For it turned out that this ancient sexton had been of the smugglers himself; and had most cunningly escaped hanging with the rest.

'There, my dear. There's your grave. See – I've tended it all these years . . .'

He paused by a patch of ground where the grass had been newly cut.

'But my treasure . . . now I can go fetch my treasure. Now I can live once more . . . now I can leave this accursed place! A – a house in London, maybe . . . a coach and pair . . . Just for my last years . . . my treasure will make up for all!'

Hastening now, he fumbled among the altar-tombs, heaving at the slabs till at last he came upon the one he sought.

'It's here! It's here!'

With a loud grinding, the slab of stone slid sideways and fell upon the ground. The old man reached within and fumbled for the hoard that had waited in the earth for eighteen years.

Bostock moved nearer. He strained to see. He sniffed the heavy air. His heart contracted in grief for the luckless sexton.

From the smugglers' hiding place, came forth only the dismal smell of rotting tea and mouldered tobacco leaf. All had crumbled away.

The old man had begun to sob. A ruinous sound.

Quite consumed with pity, Bostock laid a hand on the sexton's wasted shoulder and muttered:

'I'm sorry . . . truly sorry, sir . . .'

Whereupon the old man whirled round upon him in a sudden access of amazement and fist-shaking rage.

The hand on his shoulder, the voice in his ear had been no ghost's, but those of a mortal boy.

He beheld the fantastic Bostock. An undersized, somewhat timid grenadier whose protruding ears alone prevented his mansize cap from quite extinguishing him.

Was it to this small, mocking villain he'd opened his heart and betrayed it?

He stared – but saw no laughter in Bostock's face. Rather did he see a startled compassion that came in a gentle flood from Bostock's heart and filled up Bostock's eyes – making them to shine softly – and from thence, ran resistless down Bostock's cheeks. The boy was crying for him. The boy had partly understood, and was grieving for the wastage of his poor life, for his heart that had turned to dust – by reason of the haunting of his soul.

'What – what are you doing here, boy?'

Bostock shook his head; made to wipe his eyes, then stared, frightened, at his luminous hand and hid it behind his back.

The sexton went grey with horror – on the memory of an old, old occasion. He gave some four or five harsh, constricted cries – for all the world as if the organ that produced them was stirring after long disuse. Then he partly screamed and partly shouted:

'What have you done with your hands? What – have – you – done? Oh God, you'll die! You'll die again! He died of it! A doctor! Quick – quick! This time, I'll save you! Please God, let me save you this time!'

He reached out and seized the terrified Bostock by a cuff. Now he began to drag him, as fast as his hobble would permit, out of the churchyard and towards Brighthelmstone. And all the while, he panted: 'Let me save him – let me save him!'

Tremendous sight . . . remarked on for years afterwards by startled tavern-leavers who'd glimpsed the
bounding, limping old man and the phosphorescent
boy.

A sight never to be forgotten – least of all by Dr
Harris at whose door the sexton banged and kicked till
it was opened.

Before he could be gainsaid, he'd dragged the
wretched Bostock in and begged the doctor to try to
save him.

'What's amiss? What's amiss, then?'

'He'll die – he'll die!' wept the sexton. 'Just like the
other one!'

Then out tumbled the sexton's grim secret while the
doctor's household listened in judgement and in pity.
For though the old man had been a murderer – had
done for the foundling by his eager greed – it was plain
to all he'd paid a high price for his crime.

'This boy will be saved,' muttered Dr Harris, as he
began treating those hands inflamed by the evil ointment. 'But may God forgive you for that other one.'

Now it seemed to Bostock as he sat, with wise old
nightgowned Harris come down to be by his side, that
the night was grown suddenly warmer. The fire burned
bright – as if an obstruction had been lifted off the
chimney . . .

He was not alone in noticing this. It was remarked
on by the doctor, who diagnosed a sudden, beneficial
draught. Likewise. it was observed by the sexton – the
confessed murderer – who peered at it, then glanced
towards the window as if the cause was passing down
the street. For he nodded . . .

And though Bostock, who followed his gaze, saw
nothing but darkness, he knew that the usurping phantom had at last slipped away, its purpose achieved, its
office at full term.

So did the phantom drummer boy haunt the churchyard no more? Did it never stalk on misty Saturday
nights? And was its drum heard never again to echo
across the tumbled tombs? Yes: but only once more —
and that not so long after.

D'you remember when they buried the old sexton
at Hove? The old sexton who from that night on had
seemed to give up interest in life let alone bedevilling
the young boys who came inside his domain. It was late
on a Saturday night, and the sea mists were coming
up.

D'you remember the sound of drumming that accompanied his coffin? And the gentle beating as it was
lowered into its grave? It had a strangely forgiving
sound . . . They say it was a retreat that was being
beaten; but to Bostock and Harris it sounded more like
a welcome.

# The Monkey's Paw

W. W. JACOBS

Without, the night was cold and wet, but in the small parlour of Laburnum Villa the blinds were drawn and the fire burned brightly. Father and son were at chess; the former, who possessed ideas about the game involving radical changes, putting his king into such sharp and unnecessary perils, that it even provoked comment from the white-haired old lady knitting placidly by the fire.

'Hark at the wind,' said Mr White, who, having seen a fatal mistake after it was too late, was amiably desirous of preventing his son from seeing it.

'I'm listening,' said the latter, grimly surveying the board as he stretched out his hand. 'Check.'

'I should hardly think that he'd come tonight,' said his father, with his hand poised over the board.

'Mate,' replied the son.

'That's the worst of living so far out,' bawled Mr White, with sudden and unlooked-for violence; 'of all the beastly, slushy, out-of-the-way places to live in, this is the worst. Path's a bog, and road's a torrent. I don't know what people are thinking about. I suppose because only two houses in the road are let, they think it doesn't matter.'

'Never mind, dear,' said his wife, soothingly, 'perhaps you will win the next one.'

Mr White looked up sharply, just in time to intercept a knowing glance between mother and son. The words died away on his lips, and he hid a guilty grin in his thin grey beard.

'There he is,' said Herbert White, as the gate banged

to loudly and heavy footsteps came towards the door.

The old man rose with hospitable haste, and opening the door, was heard condoling with the new arrival. The new arrival also condoled with himself, so that Mrs White said, 'Tut, Tut!' and coughed gently as her husband entered the room, followed by a tall, burly man, beady of eye and rubicund of visage.

'Sergeant-Major Morris,' he said, introducing him.

The sergeant-major shook hands, and taking the proffered seat by the fire, watched contentedly while his host got out whisky and tumblers and stood a small copper kettle on the fire.

At the third glass his eyes got brighter, and he began to talk, the little family circle regarding with eager interest this visitor from distant parts, as he squared his broad shoulders in the chair and spoke of wild scenes and doughty deeds; of wars and plagues and strange peoples.

'Twenty-one years of it,' said Mr White, nodding at his wife and son. 'When he went away he was a slip of a youth in the warehouse. Now look at him.'

'He don't look to have taken much harm,' said Mrs White politely.

'I'd like to go to India myself,' said the old man, 'just to look around a bit, you know.'

'Better where you are,' said the sergeant-major, shaking his head. He put down the empty glass, and, sighing softly, shook his head again.

'I should like to see those old temples and fakirs and jugglers,' said the old man. 'What was that you started telling me the other day about a monkey's paw or something, Morris?'

'Nothing,' said the soldier hastily. 'Leastways nothing worth hearing.'

'Monkey's paw?' said Mrs White curiously.

'Well, it's just a bit of what you might call magic,

perhaps,' said the sergeant-major, offhandedly.

His three listeners leaned forward eagerly. The visitor absent-mindedly put his empty glass to his lips, and then set it down again. His host filled it for him.

'To look at,' said the sergeant-major, fumbling in his pocket, 'it's just an ordinary little paw, dried to a mummy.'

He took something out of his pocket and proffered it. Mrs White drew back with a grimace, but her son, taking it, examined it curiously.

'And what is there special about it?' inquired Mr White as he took it from his son, and having examined it, placed it upon the table.

'It had a spell put on it by an old fakir,' said the sergeant-major, 'a very holy man. He wanted to show that fate ruled people's lives, and that those who interfered with it did so to their sorrow. He put a spell on it so that three separate men could each have three wishes from it.'

His manner was so impressive that his hearers were conscious that their light laughter jarred somewhat.

'Well, why don't you have three, sir?' said Herbert White, cleverly.

The soldier regarded him in the way that middle age is wont to regard presumptuous youth. 'I have,' he said quietly, and his blotchy face whitened.

'And did you really have the three wishes granted?' asked Mrs White.

'I did,' said the sergeant-major, and his glass tapped against his strong teeth.

'And has anybody else wished?' persisted the old lady.

'The first man had his three wishes. Yes,' was the reply. 'I don't know what the first two were, but the third was for death. That's how I got the paw.'

His tones were so grave that a hush fell upon the group.

'If you've had your three wishes, it's no good to you now, then, Morris,' said the old man at last. 'What do you keep it for?'

The soldier shook his head. 'Fancy, I suppose,' he said slowly. 'I did have some idea of selling it, but I don't think I will. It has caused enough mischief already. Besides, people won't buy. They think it's a fairy tale, some of them; and those who do think anything of it want to try it first and pay me afterwards.'

'If you could have another three wishes,' said the old man, eyeing him keenly, 'would you have them?'

'I don't know,' said the other. 'I don't know.'

He took the paw. and dangling it between his fore-finger and thumb, suddenly threw it upon the fire. White, with a slight cry, stooped down and snatched it off.

'Better let it burn,' said the soldier solemnly.

'If you don't want it, Morris,' said the other, 'give it to me.'

'I won't,' said his friend doggedly. 'I threw it on the fire. If you keep it, don't blame me for what happens. Pitch it on the fire again, like a sensible man.'

The other shook his head and examined his new possession closely. 'How do you do it?' he inquired.

'Hold it up in your right hand and wish aloud,' said the sergeant-major, 'but I warn you of the conse-quences.'

'Sounds like *Arabian Nights*,' said Mrs White, as she rose and began to set the supper. 'Don't you think you might wish for four pairs of hands for me?'

Her husband drew the talisman from his pocket, and then all three burst into laughter as the sergeant-major, with a look of alarm on his face, caught him by the arm.

'If you must wish,' he said gruffly, 'wish for something sensible.'

Mr White dropped it back in his pocket, and placing chairs, motioned his friend to the table. In the business of supper the talisman was partly forgotten, and afterwards the three sat listening in an enthralled fashion to a second instalment of the soldier's adventures in India.

'If the tale about the monkey's paw is not more truthful than those he has been telling us,' said Herbert, as the door closed behind their guest, just in time to catch the last train, 'we shan't get much out of it.'

'Did you give him anything for it, Father?' inquired Mrs White, regarding her husband closely.

'A trifle,' said he, colouring slightly. 'He didn't want it, but I made him take it. And he pressed me again to throw it away.'

'Likely,' said Herbert, with pretended horror. 'Why, we're going to be rich, and famous and happy. Wish to be an Emperor, Father, to begin with; then you can't be henpecked.'

He darted round the table, pursued by the maligned Mrs White with an antimacassar.

Mr White took the paw from his pocket and eyed it dubiously. 'I don't know what to wish for, and that's a fact,' he said, slowly. 'It seems to me I've got all I want.'

'If you only cleared the house, you'd be quite happy, wouldn't you?' said Herbert, with his hand on his shoulder. 'Well, wish for two hundred pounds then; that'll just do it.'

His father, smiling shamefacedly at his own credulity, held up the talisman, as his son, with a solemn face, somewhat marred by a wink at his mother, sat down at the piano and struck a few impressive chords.

'I wish for two hundred pounds,' said the old man distinctly.

A fine crash from the piano greeted the words, interrupted by a shuddering cry from the old man. His wife and son ran towards him.

'It moved,' he cried, with a glance of disgust at the object as it lay on the floor.

'As I wished, it twisted in my hand like a snake.'

'Well, I don't see the money,' said his son, as he picked it up and placed it on the table, 'and I bet I never shall.'

'It must have been your fancy, Father,' said his wife, regarding him anxiously.

He shook his head. 'Never mind, though; there's no harm done, but it gave me a shock all the same.'

They sat down by the fire again while the two men finished their pipes. Outside, the wind was higher than ever, and the old man started nervously at the sound of a door banging upstairs. A silence unusual and depressing settled upon all three, which lasted until the old couple arose to retire for the night.

'I expect you'll find the cash tied up in a big bag in the middle of your bed,' said Herbert, as he bade them goodnight, 'and something horrible squatting up on top of your wardrobe watching you as you pocket your ill-gotten gains.'

He sat alone in the darkness, gazing at the dying fire, and seeing faces in it. The last face was so horrible and so simian that he gazed at it in amazement. It got so vivid that, with a little uneasy laugh, he felt on the table for a glass containing a little water to throw over it. His hand grasped the monkey's paw, and with a little shiver he wiped his hand on his coat and went up to bed.

In the brightness of the wintry sun next morning as it streamed over the breakfast table, he laughed at his fears. There was an air of prosaic wholesomeness about the room which it had lacked on the previous night, and the dirty, shrivelled little paw was pitched on the sideboard with a carelessness which betokened no great belief in its virtues.

'I suppose all old soldiers are the same,' said Mrs White. 'The idea of our listening to such nonsense! How could wishes be granted in these days? And if they could, how could two hundred pounds hurt you, Father?'

'Might drop on his head from the sky,' said the frivolous Herbert.

'Morris said the things happened so naturally,' said his father, 'that you might if you so wished attribute it to coincidence.'

'Well, don't break into the money before I come back,' said Herbert as he rose from the table. 'I'm afraid it'll turn you into a mean, avaricious man, and we shall have to disown you.'

His mother laughed, and followed him to the door, watched him down the road; and returning to the breakfast table, was very merry at the expense of her husband's credulity. All of which did not prevent her from scurrying to the door at the postman's knock, nor prevent her from referring somewhat shortly to retired sergeant-majors of bibulous habits when she found that the post brought a tailor's bill.

'Herbert will have some more of his funny remarks, I expect, when he comes home,' she said, as they sat at dinner.

'I dare say,' said Mr White, pouring himself out some beer, 'but for all that, the thing moved in my hand; that I'll swear to.'

'You thought it did,' said the old lady soothingly.

'I say it did,' replied the other. 'There was no thought about it; I had just – What's the matter?'

His wife made no reply. She was watching the mysterious movements of a man outside, who, peering in an undecided fashion at the house, appeared to be trying to make up his mind to enter. In mental connection with the two hundred pounds, she noticed that the stranger was well dressed, and wore a silk hat of glossy newness. Three times he paused at the gate, and then walked on again. The fourth time he stood with his hand upon it, and then with sudden resolution flung it open and walked up the path. Mrs White at the same moment placed her hands behind her, and hurriedly unfastening the strings of her apron, put that useful article of apparel beneath the cushion of her chair.

She brought the stranger, who seemed ill at ease, into the room. He gazed at her furtively, and listened in a preoccupied fashion as the old lady apologized for the appearance of the room, and her husband's coat, a garment which he usually reserved for the garden. She then waited as patiently as her sex would permit, for him to broach his business, but he was at first strangely silent.

'I – was asked to call,' he said at last, and stooped and picked a piece of cotton from his trousers. 'I come from "Maw and Meggins".'

The old lady started. 'Is anything the matter?' she asked breathlessly. 'Has anything happened to Herbert? What is it?'

Her husband interposed. 'There, there, Mother,' he said hastily. 'Sit down and don't jump to conclusions. You've not brought bad news, I'm sure, sir;' and he eyed the other wistfully.

'I'm sorry –' began the visitor.

'Is he hurt?' demanded the mother wildly.

The visitor bowed in assent. 'Badly hurt,' he said quietly, 'but he is not in any pain.'

'Oh, thank God!' said the old woman, clasping her hands. 'Thank God for that! Thank –'

She broke off suddenly as the sinister meaning of the assurance dawned upon her, and she saw the awful confirmation of her fears in the other's averted face. She caught her breath, and turning to her slower-witted husband, laid her trembling old hand upon his. There was a long silence.

'He was caught in the machinery,' said the visitor at length in a low voice.

'Caught in the machinery,' repeated Mr White in a dazed fashion, 'yes.'

He sat staring blankly out at the window, and taking his wife's hand between his own, pressed it as he had been wont to do in their old courting days nearly forty years before.

'He was the only one left to us,' he said, turning gently to the visitor. 'It is hard.'

The other coughed, and rising, walked slowly to the window. 'The firm wished me to convey their sincere sympathy with you in your great loss,' he said without looking round. 'I beg that you will understand I am only their servant and merely obeying orders.'

There was no reply; the old woman's face was white, her eyes staring, and her breath inaudible; and on the husband's face was a look such as his friend the sergeant might have carried into his first action.

'I was to say that Maw and Meggins disclaim all responsibility,' continued the other. 'They admit no liability at all, but in consideration of your son's services, they wish to present you with a certain sum as compensation.'

Mr White dropped his wife's hand, and rising to his feet, gazed with a look of horror at his visitor. His dry lips shaped the words, 'How much?'

'Two hundred pounds,' was the answer.

Unconscious of his wife's shriek, the old man smiled faintly, put out his hands like a senseless man, and dropped, a senseless heap, to the floor.

In the huge new cemetery, some two miles distant, the old people buried their dead, and came back to a house steeped in shadow and silence. It was all over so quickly that at first they could hardly realize it, and remained in a state of expectation as though of something else to happen – something else which was to lighten this load, too heavy for old hearts to bear.

But the days passed, and expectation gave place to resignation – the hopeless resignation of the old, sometimes miscalled apathy. Sometimes, they hardly exchanged a word, for now they had nothing to talk about, and their days were long to weariness.

It was about a week after, that the old man, waking suddenly in the night, stretched out his hand and found himself alone. The room was in darkness, and the sound of subdued weeping came from the window. He raised himself in bed and listened.

'Come back,' he said, tenderly. 'You will be cold.'

'It is colder for my son,' said the old woman, and wept afresh.

The sound of her sobs died away on his ears. The bed was warm, and his eyes heavy with sleep. He dozed fitfully and then slept until a sudden wild cry from his wife awoke him with a start.

'*The paw*!' she cried wildly. 'The monkey's paw!'

He started up in alarm. 'Where? Where is it? What's the matter?'

She came stumbling across the room towards him. 'I want it,' she said quietly. 'You've not destroyed it?'

'It's in the parlour, on the bracket,' he replied, marvelling. 'Why?'

She cried and laughed together, and bending over, kissed his cheek.

'I only just thought of it,' she said, hysterically. 'Why

didn't I think of it before? Why didn't *you* think of it?'

'Think of what?' he questioned.

'The other two wishes,' she replied, rapidly. 'We've only had one.'

'Was not that enough?' he demanded fiercely.

'No,' she cried triumphantly; 'we'll have one more. Go down and get it quickly, and wish our boy alive again.'

The man sat up in bed and flung the bedclothes from his quaking limbs. 'Good God, you are mad!' he cried aghast.

'Get it,' she panted, 'get it quickly, and wish – Oh, my boy, my boy!'

Her husband struck a match and lit the candle. 'Get back to bed,' he said unsteadily. 'You don't know what you are saying.'

'We had the first wish granted,' said the old woman, feverishly; 'why not the second?'

'A coincidence,' stammered the old man.

'Go and get it and wish,' cried his wife, quivering with excitement.

The old man turned and regarded her, and his voice shook. 'He has been dead ten days, and besides he – I would not tell you else, but – I could only recognize him by his clothing. If he was too terrible for you to see then, how now?'

'Bring him back,' cried the old woman, and dragged him towards the door. 'Do you think I fear the child I have nursed?'

He went down in the darkness, and felt his way to the parlour, and then to the mantelpiece. The talisman was in its place, and a horrible fear that the unspoken wish might bring his mutilated son before him ere he could escape from the room seized upon him, and he caught his breath as he found that he had lost the direction of the door. His brow cold with sweat, he felt his way round the table, and groped along the wall until he found himself in the small passage with the unwholesome thing in his hand.

Even his wife's face seemed changed as he entered the room. It was white and expectant, and to his fears seemed to have an unnatural look upon it. He was afraid of her.

'*Wish*,' she cried in a strong voice.

'It is foolish and wicked,' he faltered.

'*Wish*!' repeated his wife.

He raised his hand. 'I wish my son alive again.'

The talisman fell to the floor, and he regarded it fearfully. Then he sank trembling into a chair as the old woman, with burning eyes, walked to the window and raised the blind.

He sat until he was chilled with the cold, glancing occasionally at the figure of the old woman peering through the window. The candle-end, which had burned below the rim of the china candlestick, was throwing pulsating shadows on the ceiling and walls, until, with a flicker larger than the rest, it expired. The old man, with an unspeakable sense of relief at the failure of the talisman, crept back to his bed, and a minute or two afterwards the old woman came silently and apathetic-ally beside him.

Neither spoke, but lay silently listening to the ticking of the clock. A stair creaked, and a squeaky mouse scurried noisily through the wall. The darkness was oppressive, and after lying for some time, screwing up his courage, he took the box of matches, and striking one, went downstairs for a candle.

At the foot of the stairs the match went out, and he paused to strike another; and at the same moment a knock, so quiet and stealthy as to be scarcely audible, sounded on the front door.

The matches fell from his hand and spilled in the

passage. He stood motionless, his breath suspended until the knock was repeated. Then he turned and fled swiftly back to his room, and closed the door behind him. A third knock sounded through the house.

'What's that?' cried the old woman, starting up.

'A rat,' said the old man in shaking tones, ' – a rat. It passed me on the stairs.'

His wife sat up in bed listening. A loud knock resounded through the house.

'It's Herbert!' she screamed. 'It's Herbert!'

She ran to the door, but her husband was before her, and catching her by the arm, held her tightly.

'What are you going to do?' he whispered hoarsely.

'It's my boy; it's Herbert!' she cried, struggling mechanically. 'I forgot it was two miles away. What are you holding me for? Let go. I must open the door.'

'For God's sake don't let it in,' cried the old man, trembling.

'You're afraid of your own son,' she cried, struggling. 'Let me go. I'm coming, Herbert; I'm coming.'

There was another knock, and another. The old woman with a sudden wrench broke free and ran from the room. Her husband followed to the landing, and called after her appealingly as she hurried downstairs. He heard the chain rattle back and the bottom bolt drawn slowly and stiffly from the socket. Then the old woman's voice, strained and panting.

'The bolt,' she cried loudly. 'Come down. I can't reach it.'

But her husband was on his hands and knees groping wildly on the floor in search of the paw. If he could only find it before the thing outside got in. A perfect fusillade of knocks reverberated through the house, and he heard the scraping of a chair as his wife put it down in the passage against the door. He heard the creaking of the bolt as it came slowly back, and at the same moment he found the monkey's paw, and frantically breathed his third and last wish.

The knocking ceased suddenly, although the echoes of it were still in the house. He heard the chair drawn back, and the door opened. A cold wind rushed up the staircase, and a long loud wail of disappointment and misery from his wife gave him the courage to run down to her side, and then to the gate beyond. The street lamp flickering opposite shone on a quiet and deserted road.

# Feet Foremost

L.  P.  HARTLEY

The house warming at Low Threshold Hall was not an
event that affected many people. The local newspaper,
however, had half a column about it, and one or two
daily papers supplemented the usual August dearth of
topics with pictures of the house. They were all taken
from the same angle, and showed a long, low building
in the Queen Anne style flowing away from a square
tower on the left which was castellated and obviously
of much earlier date, the whole structure giving somewhat the impression to a casual glance of a domesti-
cated church, or even of a small railway train that had
stopped dead on finding itself in a park. Beneath the
photograph was written something like 'Suffolk Manor
House re-occupied after a hundred and fifty years', and,
in one instance, 'Inset (L.) Mr Charles Ampleforth, owner
of Low Threshold Hall; (R.) Sir George Willings, the
architect responsible for the restoration of this interesting medieval relic.' Mr Ampleforth's handsome, slightly
Disraelian head, nearly spiked on his own flagpole,
smiled congratulations at the grey hair and rounded
features of Sir George Willings who, suspended like a
bubble above the Queen Anne wing, discreetly smiled
back.

To judge from the photograph, time had dealt gently
with Low Threshold Hall. Only a trained observer could
have told how much of the original fabric had been
renewed. The tower looked particularly convincing.
While as for the gardens sloping down to the stream
which bounded the foreground of the picture – they
had that old-world air which gardens so quickly ac-

quire. To see those lush lawns and borders as a meadow, that mellow brickwork under scaffolding, needed a strong effort of the imagination.

But the guests assembled in Mr Ampleforth's drawing-room after dinner and listening to their host as, not for the first time, he enlarged upon the obstacles faced and overcome in the work of restoration, found it just as hard to believe that the house was old. Most of them had been taken to see it, at one time or another, in process of reconstruction; yet even within a few days of its completion, how unfinished a house looks! Its habitability seems determined in the last few hours. Magdalen Winthrop, whose beautiful, expressive face still (to her hostess's sentimental eye) bore traces of the slight disappointment she had suffered earlier in the evening, felt as if she were in an Aladdin's palace. Her glance wandered appreciatively from the Samarcand rugs to the pale green walls, and dwelt with pleasure on the high shallow arch, flanked by slender columns, the delicate lines of which were emphasized by the darkness of the hall behind them. It all seemed so perfect and so new; not only every sign of decay but the very sense of age had been banished. How absurd not to be able to find a single grey hair, so to speak, in a house that had stood empty for a hundred and fifty years! Her eyes, still puzzled, came to rest on the company, ranged in an irregular circle round the fireplace.

'What's the matter, Maggie?' said a man at her side, obviously glad to turn the conversation away from bricks and mortar. 'Looking for something?'

Mrs Ampleforth, whose still lovely skin under the abundant white hair made her face look like a rose in snow, bent forward over the cream-coloured satin bedspread she was embroidering and smiled. 'I was only thinking,' said Maggie, turning to her host whose recital had paused but not died upon his lips, 'how surprised the owls and bats would be if they could come in and see the change in their old home.'

'Oh, I do hope they won't,' cried a high female voice from the depths of a chair whose generous proportions obscured the speaker.

'Don't be such a baby, Eileen,' said Maggie's neighbour in tones that only a husband could have used. 'Wait till you see the family ghost.'

'Ronald, please! Have pity on my poor nerves!' The upper half of a tiny, childish, imploring face peered like a crescent moon over the rim of the chair.

'If there is a ghost,' said Maggie, afraid that the original remark might be construed as a criticism, 'I envy him his beautiful surroundings. I would willingly take his place.'

'Hear, hear,' agreed Ronald. 'A very happy haunting-ground. Is there a ghost, Charles?'

There was a pause. They all looked at their host.

'Well,' said Mr Ampleforth, who rarely spoke except after a pause and never without a slight impressiveness of manner, 'there is and there isn't.'

The silence grew even more respectful.

'The ghost of Low Threshold Hall,' Mr Ampleforth continued, 'is no ordinary ghost.'

'It wouldn't be,' muttered Ronald in an aside Maggie feared might be audible.

'It is for one thing,' Mr Ampleforth pursued, 'exceedingly considerate.'

'Oh, how?' exclaimed two or three voices.

'It only comes by invitation.'

'Can anyone invite it?'

'Yes, anyone.'

There was nothing Mr Ampleforth liked better than answering questions; he was evidently enjoying himself now.

'How is the invitation delivered?' Ronald asked.

'Does one telephone, or does one send a card: "Mrs Ampleforth requests the pleasure of Mr Ghost's company on – well – what is tomorrow? – the eighteenth August, Moaning and Groaning and Chain Rattling, R.S.V.P.?" '

'That would be a sad solecism,' said Mr Ampleforth. 'The ghost of Low Threshold Hall is a lady.'

'Oh,' cried Eileen's affected little voice, 'I'm so thankful, I should be much less frightened of a female phantom.'

'She hasn't attained years of discretion,' Mr Ampleforth said. 'She was only sixteen when – '

'Then she's not "out"?'

'Not in the sense you mean. I hope she's not "out" in any sense,' said Mr Ampleforth, with grim facetiousness.

There was a general shudder.

'Well, I'm glad we can't ask her to an evening party,' observed Ronald. 'A ghost at tea-time is much less alarming. Is she what is called a "popular" girl?'

'I'm afraid not.'

'Then why do people invite her?'

'They don't realize what they're doing.'

'A kind of pig in a poke business, what? But you haven't told us yet how we're to get hold of the little lady.'

'That's quite simple,' said Mr Ampleforth readily. 'She comes to the door.'

The drawing-room clock began to strike eleven, and no one spoke till it had finished.

'She comes to the door,' said Ronald with an air of deliberation, 'and then – don't interrupt, Eileen, I'm in charge of the cross-examination – she – she hangs about – '

'She waits to be asked inside.'

'I suppose there is a time-honoured formula of invitation: "Sweet Ermyntrude, in the name of the master of the house, I bid thee welcome to Low Threshold Hall. There's no step, so you can walk straight in." Charles, much as I admire your house, I do think it's incomplete without a doorstep. A ghost could just sail in.'

'There you make a mistake,' said Mr Ampleforth impressively. 'Our ghost cannot enter the house unless she is lifted across the threshold.'

'Like a bride,' exclaimed Magdalen.

'Yes,' said Mr Ampleforth. 'Because she came as a bride.' He looked round at his guests with an enigmatic smile.

They did not disappoint him. 'Now, Charlie, don't be so mysterious! Do tell us! Tell us the whole story.'

Mr Ampleforth settled himself into his chair. 'There's very little to tell,' he said, with the reassuring manner of someone who intends to tell a great deal, 'but this is the tale. In the time of the Wars of the Roses the owner of Low Theshold Hall (I need not tell you his name was not Ampleforth) married "en troisièmes noces" the daughter of a neighbouring baron much less powerful than he. Lady Elinor Stortford was sixteen when she came and did not live to see her seventeenth birthday. Her husband was a bad hat (I'm sorry to have to say so of a predecessor of mine), a very bad hat. He ill-treated her, drove her mad with terror, and finally killed her.'

The narrator paused dramatically, but the guests felt slightly disappointed. They had heard so many stories of the kind.

'Poor thing,' said Magdalen, feeling that some comment was necessary, however flat. 'So now she haunts the place. I suppose it's the nature of ghosts to linger where they've suffered, but it seems illogical to me. I should want to go somewhere else.'

'The Lady Elinor would agree with you. The first thing she does when she gets into the house is make plans for getting out. Her visits, as far as I can gather, have generally been brief.'

'Then why does she come?' asked Eileen.

'She comes for vengeance.' Mr Ampleforth's voice dropped at the word. 'And apparently she gets it. Within a short time of her appearance, someone in the house always dies.'

'Nasty spiteful little girl,' said Ronald, concealing a yawn. 'Then how long is she in residence?'

'Until her object is accomplished.'

'Does she make a dramatic departure – in a thunderstorm or something?'

'No, she is just carried out.'

'Who carries her this time?'

'The undertaker's men. She goes out with the corpse. Though some say – '

'Oh, Charlie, do stop!' Mrs Ampleforth interrupted, bending down to gather up the corners of her bedspread. 'Eileen will never sleep. Let's go to bed.'

'No! No!' shouted Ronald. 'He can't leave off like that. I must hear the rest. My flesh was just beginning to creep.'

Mr Ampleforth looked at his wife. 'I've had my orders.'

'Well, well,' said Ronald, resigned, 'Anyhow, remember what I said. A decent fall of rain, and you'll have a foot of water under the tower there, unless you put in a doorstep.'

Mr Ampleforth looked grave. 'Oh no, I couldn't do that. That would be to invite er – er – trouble. The absence of a step was a precaution. That's how the house got its name.'

'A precaution against what?'

'Against Lady Elinor.'

'But how? I should have thought a drawbridge would have been more effective?'

'Lord Deadham's immediate heirs thought the same. According to the story they put every material obstacle they could to bar the lady's path. You can still see in the tower the grooves which contained the portcullis. And there was a flight of stairs so steep and dangerous they couldn't be used without risk to life and limb. But that only made it easier for Lady Elinor.'

'How did it?'

'Why, don't you see, everyone who came to the house, friends and strangers alike, had to be helped over the threshold! There was no way of distinguishing between them. At last when so many members of the family had been killed off that it was threatened with extinction, someone conceived a brilliant idea. Can you guess what it was, Maggie?'

'They removed all the barriers and levelled the threshold, so that any stranger who came to the door and asked to be helped into the house was refused admittance.'

'Exactly, and the plan seems to have worked remarkably well.'

'But the family did die out in the end,' observed Maggie.

'Yes,' said Mr Ampleforth, 'soon after the middle of the eighteenth century. The best human plans are fallible, and Lady Elinor was very persistent.'

He held the company with his glittering raconteur's eye.

But Mrs Ampleforth was standing up. 'Now, now,' she said. 'I gave you twenty minutes' grace. It will soon be midnight. Come along, Maggie, you must be tired after your journey. Let me light you a candle.' She took the girl's arm and piloted her into the comparative darkness of the hall. 'I think they must be on this table,' she said, her fingers groping; 'I don't know the house myself yet. We ought to have had a light put here. But it's one of Charlie's little economies to have as few lights as possible. I'll tell him about it. But it takes so long to get anything done in this out-of-the-way spot. My dear, nearly three miles to the nearest clergyman, four to the nearest doctor! Ah, here we are, I'll light some for the others. Charlie is still holding forth about Lady Elinor. You didn't mind that long recital?' she added, as, accompanied by their shadows, they walked up the stairs. 'Charlie does so love an audience. And you don't feel uncomfortable or anything? I am always so sorry for Lady Elinor, poor soul, if she ever existed. Oh, and I wanted to say we were so disappointed about Antony. I feel we got you down today on false pretences. Something at the office kept him. But he's coming tomorrow. When is the wedding to be, dearest?'

'In the middle of September.'

'Quite soon, now. I can't tell you how excited I am about it. I think he's such a dear. You both are. Now which is your way, left, right or middle? I'm ashamed to say I've forgotten.'

Maggie considered. 'I remember; it's to the left.'

'In that black abyss? Oh, darling, I forgot; do you feel equal to going on the picnic tomorrow? We shan't get back till five. It'll be a long day; I'll stay at home with you if you like – I'm tired of ruins.'

'I'd love to go.'

'Goodnight, then.'

'Goodnight.'

In the space of ten minutes the two men, left to themselves, had succeeded in transforming the elegant Queen Mary drawing-room into something that looked and smelt like a bar-parlour.

'Well,' observed Ronald who, more than his host, had been responsible for the room's deterioration, 'time to turn in. I have a rendezvous with Lady Elinor. By the way, Charles,' he went on, 'have you given the servants instructions in anti-Elinor technique – told them only to admit visitors who can enter the house under their own steam, so to speak?'

'Mildred thought it wisest, and I agree with her,' said Mr Ampleforth, 'to tell the servants nothing at all. It might unsettle them, and we shall have hard work to keep them as it is.'

'Perhaps you're right,' said Ronald. 'Anyhow it's no part of their duty to show the poor lady out. Charles, what were you going to say that wasn't fit for ears polite when Mildred stopped you?'

Mr Ampleforth reflected, 'I wasn't aware . . .'

'Oh, yes, she nipped your smoking-room story in the bud. I asked, "Who carried Lady Elinor out?" and you said, "The undertaker's men, she goes out with the corpse", and you were going to say something else when you were called to order.'

'Oh, I remember,' said Mr Ampleforth. 'It was such a small point. I couldn't imagine why Mildred objected. According to one story, she doesn't go out *with* the corpse, she goes out *in* it.'

Ronald pondered. 'Don't see much difference, do you?'

'I can't honestly say I do.'

'Women are odd creatures,' Ronald said. 'So long.'

The cat stood by the library door, miaowing. Its intention was perfectly plain. First it had wanted to go out; then it strolled up and down outside the window, demanding to come in; now it wanted to go out again. For the third time in half an hour Antony Fairfield rose from his comfortable chair to do its bidding. He opened the door gently – all his movements were gentle; but the cat scuttled ignominiously out, as though he had kicked it. Antony looked round. How could he defend himself from disturbance without curtailing the cat's liberty of movement? He might leave the window and the door open, to give the animal freedom of exit and entrance: though he hated sitting in a room with the door open, he was prepared to make the sacrifice. But he couldn't leave the window open because the rain would come in and spoil Mrs Ampleforth's beautiful silk cushions. Heavens, how it rained! Too bad for the farmers, thought Antony, whose mind was always busying itself with other people's misfortunes. The crops had been looking so well as he drove in the sunshine from the station, and now this sudden storm would beat everything down. He arranged his chair so that he could see the window and not keep the cat waiting if she felt like paying him another visit. The pattering of the rain soothed him. Half an hour and they would be back – Maggie would be back. He tried to visualize their faces, all so well known to him; but the experiment was not successful. Maggie's image kept ousting the others; it even appeared, somewhat grotesquely, on the top of Ronald's well-tailored shoulders. They mustn't find me asleep, thought Antony; I should look too middle-aged. So he picked up the newspaper from the floor and turned to the cross-word puzzle. 'Nine points of the law' in ten letters. That was a very easy one: 'Possession.' Possession, thought Anthony; I must put that down. But as he had no pencil and was too sleepy to get one, he repeated the word over and over again: Possession, Possession. It worked like a charm. He fell asleep and dreamed.

In his dream he was still in the library, but it was night and somehow his chair had got turned around so that he no longer faced the window, but he knew that the cat was there, asking to come in; only someone – Maggie – was trying to persuade him not to let it in. 'It's not a cat at all,' she kept saying; 'it's a Possession. I can see its nine points and they're very sharp.' But he knew that she was mistaken, and really meant nine lives, which all cats have : so he thrust her aside and ran to the window and opened it. It was too dark to see, so he put out his hand where he thought the cat's body would be, expecting to feel the warm fur; but what met his hand was not warm, nor was it fur . . . He woke with a start to see the butler standing in front of him. The room was flooded with sunshine.

'Oh, Rundle,' he cried, 'I was asleep. Are they back?'

The butler smiled.

'No, sir, but I expect them every minute now.'

'But you wanted me?'

'Well, sir, there's a young lady called, and I said the master was out, but she said could she speak to the gentleman in the library? She must have seen you, sir, as she passed the window.'

'How very odd. Does she know me?'

'That was what she said, sir. She talks rather funny.'

'All right. I'll come.'

Antony followed the butler down the long corridor. When they reached the tower their footsteps ran on the paved floor. A considerable pool of water, the result of the recent heavy shower, had formed on the flagstones near the doorway. The door stood open, letting in a flood of light, but of the caller there was no sign.

'She was here a moment ago,' the butler said.

'Ah, I see her,' cried Antony. 'At least, isn't that her reflected in the water? She must be leaning against the door-post.'

'That's right,' said Rundle. 'Mind the puddle, sir. Let me give you a hand. I'll have all this cleared up before they come back.'

Five minutes later two cars, closely following each other, pulled up at the door, and the picnic party tumbled out.

'Dear me, how wet!' cried Mrs Ampleforth, standing in the doorway. 'What has happened, Rundle? Has there been a flood?'

'It was much worse before you arrived, madam,' said the butler, disappointed that his exertions with mop, floor-cloth, scrubbing-brush and pail were being so scantily recognized. 'You could have sailed a boat on it. Mr Anthony, he . . .'

'Oh, has he arrived? Antony's here, isn't that splendid?'

'Antony!' they all shouted. 'Come out! Come down! Where are you?'

'I bet he's asleep, the lazy devil,' remarked Ronald.

'No, sir,' said the butler, at last able to make himself heard. 'Mr Antony's in the drawing-room with a lady.'

Mrs Ampleforth's voice broke the silence that succeeded this announcement.

'With a lady, Rundle? Are you sure?'

'Well, madam, she's hardly more than a girl.'

'I always thought Antony was that sort of man,' observed Ronald. 'Maggie, you'd better . . .'

'It's too odd,' interposed Mrs Ampleforth hastily, 'who in the world can she be?'

'I don't see there's anything odd in someone calling on us,' said Mr Ampleforth. 'What's her name, Rundle?'

'She didn't give a name, sir.'

'That is rather extraordinary. Antony is so impulsive and kind-hearted. I hope – ah, here he is.'

Antony came towards them along the passage, smiling and waving his hands. When the welcoming and handshaking were over:

'We were told you had a visitor,' said Mrs Ampleforth.

'Yes,' said Ronald. 'I'm afraid we arrived at the wrong moment.'

Antony laughed and then looked puzzled. 'Believe me, you didn't,' he said. 'You almost saved my life. She speaks such a queer dialect when she speaks at all, and I had reached the end of my small talk. But she's rather interesting. Do come along and see her: I left her in the library.' They followed Antony down the passage. When they reached the door he said to Mrs Ampleforth:

'Shall I go in first? She may be shy at meeting so many people.'

He went in. A moment later they heard his voice raised in excitement.

'Mildred! I can't find her! She's gone!'

Tea had been cleared away, but Antony's strange visitor was still the topic of conversation. 'I can't understand it,' he was saying, not for the first time. 'The windows were shut, and if she'd gone by the door we must have seen her.'

'Now, Antony,' said Ronald severely, 'let's hear the whole story again. Remember, you are accused of smuggling into the house a woman of doubtful reputation. Furthermore the prosecution alleges that when you heard us call (we were shouting ourselves hoarse, but he didn't come at once, you remember) you popped her out of that window and came out to meet us, smiling sheepishly, and feebly gesticulating. What do you say?'

'I've told you everything,' said Antony. 'I went to the door and found her leaning against the stonework. Her eyes were shut. She didn't move and I thought she must be ill. So I said, "Is anything the matter?" and she looked up and said, "My leg hurts". Then I saw by the way she was standing that her hip must have been

broken once and never properly set. I asked her where she lived, and she didn't seem to understand me; so I changed the form of the question, as one does on the telephone, and asked where she came from, and she said, "A little further down", meaning down the hill, I suppose.'

'Probably from one of the men's cottages,' said Mrs Ampleforth.

'I asked if it was far, and she said "No", which was obvious, otherwise her clothes would have been wet and they weren't, only a little muddy. She even had some mud on her medieval bridesmaid's head-dress (I can't describe her clothes again, Mildred; you know how bad I am at that). So I asked if she'd had a fall, and she said, "No, I got dirty coming up", or so I understood her. It wasn't easy to understand her: I suppose she talked the dialect of these parts. I concluded (you all say you would have known long before) that she was a little mad, but I didn't like to leave her looking so rotten, so I said, "Won't you come in and rest a minute?" Then I wished I hadn't.'

'Because she looked so pleased?'

'Oh, much more than pleased. And she said, "I hope you won't live to regret it", rather as though she hoped I should. And then I only meant just to take her hand, because of the water, you know, and she was lame . . .'

'And instead she flung herself into the poor fellow's arms . . .'

'Well, it amounted to that. I had no option! So I carried her across and put her down and she followed me here, walking better than I expected. A minute later you arrived; I asked her to wait and she didn't. That's all.'

'I should like to have seen Antony doing the St Christopher act!' said Ronald. 'Was she heavy, old boy?'

Antony shifted his chair. 'Oh, no,' he said, 'not at all. Not at all heavy.' Unconsciously he stretched his arms out in front of him, as though testing an imaginary weight. 'I see my hands are grubby,' he said with an expression of distaste. 'I must go and wash them. I won't be a moment, Maggie.'

That night, after dinner, there was some animated conversation in the servants' hall.

'Did you hear any more, Mr Rundle?' asked a housemaid of the butler, who had returned from performing his final office at the dinner-table.

'I did,' said Rundle, 'but I don't know that I ought to tell you.'

'It won't make any difference, Mr Rundle, whether you do or don't. I'm going to give in my notice tomorrow. I won't stay in a haunted house. We've been lured here. We ought to have been warned.'

'They certainly meant to keep it from us,' said Rundle. 'I myself had put two and two together after seeing Lady Elinor; what Wilkins said when he came in for his tea only confirmed my suspicions. No gardener can ever keep a still tongue in his head. It's a pity.'

'Wouldn't you have told us yourself, Mr Rundle?' asked the cook.

'I should have used my discretion,' the butler replied. 'When I informed Mr Ampleforth that I was no longer in ignorance, he said, "I rely on you, Rundle, not to say anything which might alarm the staff".'

'Mean, I call it,' exclaimed the kitchen-maid indignantly. 'They want to have all the fun and leave us to die like rats in a trap.'

Rundle ignored the interruption.

'I told Mr Ampleforth that Wilkins had been talebearing and would he excuse it in an outdoor servant, but unfortunately we were now in possession of the facts.'

'That's why they talked about it at dinner,' said the maid who helped Rundle to wait.

'They didn't really throw the mask off till after you'd gone, Lizzie,' said the butler. 'Then I began to take part in the conversation.'

He paused for a moment.

'Mr Ampleforth asked me whether anything was missing from the house, and I was able to reply, "No, everything was in order".'

'What else did you say?' inquired the cook.

'I made the remark that the library window wasn't fastened, as they thought, but only closed, and Mrs Turnbull laughed and said, "Perhaps it's only a thief, after all", but the others didn't think she could have got through the window anyhow, unless her lameness was all put on. And then I told them what the police had said about looking out for a suspicious character.'

'Did they seem frightened?' asked the cook.

'Not noticeably,' replied the butler. 'Mrs Turnbull said she hoped the gentlemen wouldn't stay long over their port. Mr Ampleforth said, "No, they have had a full day, and would be glad to go to bed." Mrs Ampleforth asked Miss Winthrop if she wanted to change her bedroom, but she said she didn't. Then Mr Fairfield asked if he could have some iodine for his hand, and Miss Winthrop said she would fetch him some. She wanted to bring it after dinner, but he said, "Oh, to-morrow morning will do, darling". He seemed rather quiet.'

'What's he done to his hand?'

'I saw the mark when he took his coffee. It was like a burn.'

'They didn't say they were going to shut the house up, or anything?'

'Oh, lord, no. There's going to be a party next week. They'll all have to stay for that.'

'I never knew such people,' said the kitchen-maid. 'They'd rather die, and us too, than miss their pleasures. I wouldn't stay another day if I wasn't forced. When you think she may be here in this very room, listening to us!' She shuddered.

'Don't you worry, my girl,' said Rundle, rising from his chair with a gesture of dismissal. 'She won't waste her time listening to you.'


'We really might be described as a set of crocks,' said Mr Ampleforth to Maggie, after luncheon the following day. 'You, poor dear, with your headache; Eileen with her nerves; I with – well – a touch of rheumatism; Antony with his bad arm.'

Maggie looked troubled.

'My headache is nothing, but I'm afraid Antony isn't very well.'

'He's gone to lie down, hasn't he?'

'Yes.'

'The best thing. I telephoned for the doctor to come this evening. He can have a look at all of us, ha! ha! Meanwhile, where will you spend the afternoon? I think the library's the coolest place on a stuffy day like this and I did want you to see my collection of books about Low Threshold – my Thresholdiana I call them.'

Maggie followed him into the library.

'Here they are. Most of them are nineteenth-century books, publications of the Society of Antiquaries, and so on; but some are older. I got a little man in Charing Cross Road to hunt them out for me; I haven't had time to read them all myself.'

Maggie took a book at random from the shelves.

'Now I'll leave you,' said her host. 'And later in the afternoon I know that Eileen would appreciate a little visit. Ronald says it's nothing, just a little nervous upset, stomach trouble. Between ourselves, I fear Lady Elinor is to blame.'

Maggie opened the book. It was called *An Enquiry into the Recent Tragicall Happenings at Low Threshold Hall in the County of Suffolk, with some Animadversions on the Barbarous Customs of our Ancestors.* It opened with a rather tedious account of the semi-mythical origins of the Deadham family. Maggie longed to skip this, but she might have to discuss the book with Mr Ampleforth, so she ploughed on. Her persistence was rewarded by a highly coloured picture of Lady Elinor's husband and an account of the cruelties he practised on her. The story would have been too painful to read had not the author (Maggie felt) so obviously drawn upon a very vivid imagination. But suddenly her eyes narrowed. What was this?

— Once in a Drunken Fitt he so mishandled her that her thigh was broken near the hip, and her screams were so loud they were heard by the servants through three closed doores; and yet he would not summon a Chirurgeon, for (quoth he) . . .

— Lord Deadham's reason was coarse in the extreme; Maggie hastened on.

And in consequence of these Barbarities, her nature, which was soft and yielding at the first, was greatly changed, and those who sawe her now (but Pitie seal'd their lips) would have said she had a Bad Hearte.

No wonder, thought Maggie, reading with a new and painful interest how the murdered woman avenged herself on various descendants, direct and collateral, of her persecutor.

And it had been generally supposed by the vulgar that her vengeance was directed only against members of that family from which she had taken so many Causeless Hurtes; and the depraved, defective, counterfeit records of those times have lent colour to this Opinion. Whereas the truth is as I now state it, having had access to those death-bed and testamentary depositions which, preserved in ink, however faint, do greater service to verity than the relations of Pot-House Historians, enlarged by Memory and confused by Ale. Yet it is on such Testimonies that rash and sceptical Heads rely when they assert that the Lady Elinor had no hand in the later Horrid Occurrence at Low Threshold Hall, which I shall presently describe, thinking that a meer visitor and no blood relation could not be the object of her vengeance, notwithstanding the evidence of two serving-maids one at the door and one craning her neck from an upper casement, who saw him beare her in: The truth being that she maketh no distinction between persons, but whoso admits her, on him doth her vengeance fall. Seven times she hath brought death to Low Threshold Hall; Three, it is true, being members of the family, but the remaining four indifferent Persons and not connected with them, having in common only this piece of folie, that they, likewise, let her in. And in each case she hath used the same manner of attack, as those who have beheld her first a room's length, then no further than a Lover's Embrace, from her victim have 'in articulo mortis' delivered. And the moment when she is no longer seen, which to the watchers seems the Clarion and Reveille of their hopes, is in reality the knell; for she hath not withdrawn further, but approached nearer, she hath not gone out but entered in: and from her dreadful Citadel within the body rejoyces, doubtless, to see the tears and hear the groanes, of those who with Comfortable Faces (albeit with sinking Hearts), would soothe the passage of the parting Soul. Their lacrimatory effusions are balm to her wicked Minde; the sad gale and ventilation of their sighs a pleasing Zephyr to her vindictive spirit.

Maggie put down the book for a moment and stared in front of her. Then she began again to read.

Once only hath she been cheated of her Prey, and it happened thus. His Bodie was already swollen with the malignant Humours she had stirred up in him and his life despaired of when a kitchen-wench was taken with an Imposthume that bled inwardly. She being of small account and but lately arrived they did only lay her in the Strawe, charging the Physician (and he nothing loth, expecting no Glory or Profitt from attendance on such a wretched creature) not to divide his Efforts but use all his skill to save their Cousin (afterwards the twelfth Lord). Notwithstanding which precaution he did hourly get worse until sodainely a change came and he began to amend. Whereat was such rejoycing (including an Ox roasted whole) that the night was spent before they heard that the serving-maid was dead. In their Revels they gave small heed to this Event, not realizing that they owed His life to Hers; for a fellow-servant who tended the maid (out of charity) declared that her death and the cousin's recovery followed as quickly as a clock striking Two. And the Physician said it was well, for she would have died in any case.

Whereby we must conclude that the Lady Elinor,

like other Apparitions, is subject to certain Lawes. One, to abandon her Victim and seeking another tenement to transfer her vengeance, should its path be crossed by a Body yet nearer Dissolution; and another is, she cannot possess or haunt the corpse after it hath received Christian Buriall. As witness the fact that the day after the interment of the tenth Lord she again appeared at the Doore and being recognized by her inability to make the Transit was turned away and pelted. And another thing I myself believe but have no proof of is: That her power is circumscribed by the walls of the House; those victims of her Malignitie could have been saved but for the dreadful swiftness of the disease and the doctors unwillingness to move a Sicke man; otherwise how could the Termes of her Curse that she pronounced be fulfilled: 'They shall be carried out Feet Foremost'?

Maggie read no more. She walked out of the library with the book under her arm. Before going to see how Antony was, she would put it in her bedroom where no one could find it. Troubled and oppressed, she paused at the head of the stairs. Her way lay straight ahead. But her glance automatically travelled to the right where, at the far end of the passage, Antony's bedroom lay. She looked again; the door which she could only just see, was shut now. But she could swear it had closed upon a woman. There was nothing odd in that; Mildren might have gone in, or Muriel, or a servant. But all the same she could not rest. Hurriedly she changed her dress and went to Antony's room. Pausing at the door she listened and distinctly heard his voice, speaking rapidly and in a low tone; but no one seemed to reply. She got no answer to her knock, so, mustering her courage, she walked in.

The blind was down and the room half dark, and the talking continued, which increased her uneasiness. Then, as her eyes got used to the darkness, she realized, with a sense of relief, that he was talking in his sleep. She pulled up the blind a little, so that she might see his hand. The brown mark had spread, she thought, and looked rather puffy as though coffee had been injected under the skin. She felt concerned for him. He would never have gone properly to bed like that, in his pyjamas, if he hadn't felt ill, and he tossed about restlessly. Maggie bent over him. Perhaps he had been eating a biscuit; there was some gritty stuff on the pillow. She tried to scoop it up but it eluded her. She could make no sense of his mutterings, but the word 'light' came in a good deal. Perhaps he was only half asleep and wanted the blind down. At last her ears caught the sentence which was running on his lips: 'She was so light.' Light? A light woman? Browning. The words conveyed nothing to her, and not wishing to wake him she tiptoed from the room.

'The doctor doesn't seem to think seriously of any of us, Maggie, you'll be glad to hear,' said Mr Ampleforth, coming into the drawing-room about six o'clock. 'Eileen's coming down to dinner. I am to drink less port – I didn't need a doctor, alas! to tell me that. Antony's the only casualty; he's got a slight temperature, and had better stay where he is until tomorrow. The doctor thinks it is one of those damnable horse-flies; his arm is a bit swollen, that's all.'

'Has he gone?' asked Maggie quickly.

'Who, Antony?'

'No, no, the doctor.'

'Oh, I'd forgotten your poor head. No, you'll just catch him. His car's on the terrace.'

The doctor, a kindly, harassed, middle-aged man, listened patiently to Maggie's questions.

'The brown mark? Oh, that's partly the inflammation, partly the iodine – he's been applying it pretty liberally, you know; amateur physicians are all alike; feel they can't have too much of a good thing.'

'You don't think the water here's responsible? I wondered if he ought to go away.'

'The water? Oh, no. No, it's a bite all right, though I confess I can't see the place where the devil got his beak in. I'll come tomorrow, if you like, but there's really no need.'

The next morning, returning from his bath, Ronald marched into Antony's room. The blind went up with a whizz and a smack, and Antony opened his eyes.

'Good morning, old man,' said Ronald cheerfully, 'Thought I'd look in and see you. How goes the blood-poisoning? Better?'

Antony drew up his sleeve and hastily replaced it. The arm beneath was chocolate-coloured to the elbow.

'I feel pretty rotten,' he said.

'I say, that's bad luck. What's this?' added Ronald, coming nearer, 'Have you been sleeping in both beds?'

'Not to my knowledge,' murmured Antony.

'You have, though,' said Ronald. 'If this bed hasn't been slept in, it's been slept on, or lain on. That I can swear. Only a head, my boy, could have put that dent in the pillow, and only a pair of muddy – hullo! The pillow's got it, too.'

'Got what?' asked Antony drowsily.

'Well, if you ask me, it's common garden mould.'

'I'm not surprised. I feel pretty mouldy, too.'

'Well, Antony; to save your good name with the servants, I'll remove the traces.'

With characteristic vigour Ronald swept and smoothed the bed.

'Now you'll be able to look Rundle in the face.'

There was a knock at the door.

'If this is Maggie,' said Ronald, 'I'm going.'

It was, and he suited the action to the word.

'You needn't trouble to tell me, dearest,' she said, 'that you are feeling much better, because I can see that you aren't.'

Antony moved his head uneasily on the pillow.

'I don't feel very flourishing, to tell you the honest truth.'

'Listen' — Maggie tried to make her voice sound casual — 'I don't believe this is a very healthy place. Don't laugh, Antony; we're all of us more or less under the weather. I think you ought to go away.'

'My dear, don't be hysterical. One often feels rotten when one wakes up. I shall be all right in a day or two.'

'Of course you will. But all the same if you were in Sussex Square you could call in Fosbrook — and, well, I should be more comfortable.'

'But you'd be here!'

'I could stay at Pamela's.'

'But, darling, that would break up the party. I couldn't do it; and it wouldn't be fair to Mildred.'

'My angel, you're no good to the party, lying here in bed. And as long as you're here, let me warn you they won't see much of me.'

A look of irritation Maggie had never noticed before came into his face as he said, almost spitefully:

'Supposing the doctor won't allow you to come in? It may be catching, you know.'

Maggie concealed the hurt she felt.

'All the more reason for you to be out of the house.'

He pulled up the bedclothes with a gesture of annoy-ance and turned away.

'Oh, Maggie, don't keep nagging at me. You ought to be called Naggie, not Maggie.'

This was an allusion to an incident in Maggie's childhood. Her too great solicitude for a younger brother's safety had provoked the gibe. It had always wounded her, but never so much as coming from Antony's lips. She rose to go.

'Do put the bed straight,' said Antony, still with face averted. 'Otherwise they'll think you've been sleeping here.'

'What?'

'Well, Ronald said something about it.'

Maggie closed the door softly behind her. Antony was ill, of course, she must remember that. But he had been ill before, and was always an angelic patient. She went down to breakfast feeling miserable.

After breakfast, at which everyone else had been unusually cheerful, she thought of a plan. It did not prove so easy of execution as she hoped.

'But, dearest Maggie,' said Mildred, 'the village is nearly three miles away. And there's nothing to see there.'

'I love country post-offices,' said Maggie. 'They always have such amusing things.'

'There is a post-office,' admitted Mildred. 'But are you sure it isn't something we could do from here? Telephone, telegraph?'

'Perhaps there'd be a picture-postcard of the house,' said Maggie feebly.

'Oh, but Charlie has such nice ones,' Mildred protested. 'He's so house-proud, you could trust him for that. Don't leave us for two hours just to get postcards. We shall miss you so much, and think of poor Antony left alone all the morning.'

Maggie had been thinking of him.

'He'll get on all right without me,' she said lightly.

'Well, wait till the afternoon when the chauffeur or Ronald can run you over in a car. He and Charlie have gone into Norwich and won't be back till lunch.'

'I think I'll walk,' said Maggie. 'It'll do me good.'

'I managed that very clumsily,' she thought, 'so how shall I persuade Antony to tell me the address of his firm?'

To her surprise his room was empty. He must have gone away in the middle of writing a letter, for there were sheets lying about on the writing table and, what luck! an envelope addressed to Higgins & Stukeley, 312 Paternoster Row. A glance was all she really needed to memorize the address; but her eyes wandered to the litter on the table. What a mess! There were several pages of notepapers covered with figures. Antony had been making calculations and, as was his habit, decorating them with marginal illustrations. He was good at drawing faces, and he had a gift for catching a likeness. Maggie had often seen, and been gratified to see, slips of paper embellished with portraits of herself – full-face, side-face, three-quarter-face. But this face that looked out from among the figures and seemed to avoid her glance, was not hers. It was the face of a woman she had never seen before but whom she felt she would recognize anywhere, so consistent and vivid were the likenesses. Scattered among the loose leaves were the contents of Antony's pocket-book. She knew he always carried her photograph. Where was it? Seized by an impulse, she began to rummage among the papers. Ah, here it was. But it was no longer hers! With a few strokes, Antony had transformed her oval face, unlined and soft of feature, into a totally different one, a pinched face with high cheekbones, hollow cheeks, and bright hard eyes from whose corners a sheaf of fine wrinkles spread like a fan: a face with which she was already too familiar.

Unable to look at it, she turned away and saw Antony standing behind her. He seemed to have come from the bath for he carried a towel and was wearing his dressing-gown.

'Well,' he said. 'Do you think it's an improvement?'

She could not answer him, but walked over to the wash-stand, and took up the thermometer that was lying on it.

'Ought you to be walking about like that,' she said at last, 'with a temperature of a hundred?'

'Perhaps not,' he replied, making two or three goat-like skips towards the bed. 'But I feel rather full of beans this morning.'

Maggie edged away from his smile towards the door.

'There isn't anything I can do for you?'

'Not today, my darling.'

The term of endearment struck her like a blow.

Maggie sent off her telegram and turned into the village street. The fact of being able to do something had relieved her mind: already in imagination she saw Antony being packed into the Ampleforths' Daimler with rugs and hot-water bottles and herself, perhaps, seated by the driver. They were endlessly kind and would make no bones about motoring him to London. But, though her spirits were rising her body felt tired; the day was sultry, and she had hurried. Another bad night like last night, she thought, and I shall be a wreck. There was a chemist's shop over the way, and she walked in.

'Can I have some sal volatile?'

'Certainly, madam.'

She drank it and felt better.

'Oh, and have you anything in the way of a sleeping draught?'

'We have some allodanol tablets, madam.'

'I'll take them.'

'Have you a doctor's prescription?'

'No.'

'Then I'm afraid you'll have to sign the poison book. Just a matter of form.'

Maggie recorded her name, idly wondering what J. Bates, her predecessor on the list, meant to do with his cyanide of potassium.

'We must try not to worry,' said Mrs Ampleforth handing Maggie her tea, 'but I must say I'm glad the doctor has come. It relieves one of responsibility, doesn't it? Not that I feel disturbed about Antony – he was quite bright when I went to see him just before lunch. And he's been sleeping since. But I quite see what Maggie means. He doesn't seem himself. Perhaps it would be a good plan, as she suggests, to send him to London. He would have better advice there.'

Rundle came in.

'A telegram for Mr Fairfield, madam.'

'It's been telephoned: "Your presence urgently required Tuesday morning – Higgins & Stukeley." Tuesday, that's tomorrow. Everything seems to point to his going, doesn't it, Charles?'

Maggie was delighted, but a little surprised, that Mrs Ampleforth had fallen in so quickly with the plan of sending Antony home.

'Could he go today?' she asked.

'Tomorrow would be too late, wouldn't it?' said Mr Ampleforth drily. 'The car's at his disposal; he can go whenever he likes.'

Through her relief Maggie felt a little stab of pain that they were both so ready to see the last of Antony. He was generally such a popular guest.

'I could go with him,' she said.

Instantly they were up in arms. Ronald the most vehement of all. 'I'm sure Antony wouldn't want you to; you know what I mean, Maggie, it's such a long drive, in a closed car on a stuffy evening. Charlie says he'll send a man, if necessary.'

Mr Ampleforth nodded.

'But if he were ill!' cried Maggie.

The entrance of the doctor cut her short. He looked rather grave.

'I wish I could say I was satisfied with Mr Fairfield's progress,' he said, 'but I can't. The inflammation has spread up the arm as far as the shoulder, and there's some fever. His manner is odd, too, excitable and apathetic by turns.' He paused. 'I should like a second opinion.'

Mr Ampleforth glanced at his wife.

'In that case wouldn't it be better to send him to London? As a matter of fact, his firm had telegraphed for him. He could go quite comfortably in the car.'

The doctor answered immediately:

'I wouldn't advise such a course. I think it would be most unwise to move him. His firm – you must excuse me – will have to do without him for a day or two.'

'Perhaps,' suggested Maggie trembling, 'it's a matter that could be arranged at his house. They could send over someone from the office. I know they make a fuss about having him on the spot,' she concluded lamely.

'Or, Doctor,' said Mr Ampleforth, 'could you do us a very great kindness and go with him? We could telephone to his doctor to meet you, and the car would get you home by midnight.'

The doctor squared his shoulders: he was clearly one of those men whose resolution stiffens under opposition.

'I consider it would be the height of folly,' he said, 'to move him out of the house. I dare not do it on my responsibility. I will get a colleague over from Ipswich tomorrow morning. In the meantime, with your permission, I will arrange for a trained nurse to be sent tonight.'

Amid a subdued murmur of final instructions, the doctor left.

As Maggie, rather late, was walking upstairs to dress for dinner, she met Rundle. He looked anxious.

'Excuse me, miss,' he said, 'but have you seen Mr Fairfield? I've asked everyone else, and they haven't. I took up his supper half an hour ago, and he wasn't in his room. He'd got his dress clothes out, but they were all on the bed except the stiff shirt.'

'Have you been to look since?' asked Maggie.

'No, miss.'

'I'll go and see.'

She tiptoed along the passage to Antony's door. A medley of sounds, footsteps, drawers being opened and shut, met her ears.

She walked back to Rundle. 'He's in there all right,' she said. 'Now I must make haste and dress.'

A few minutes later a bell rang in the kitchen.

'Who's that?'

'Miss Winthrop's room,' said the cook. 'Hurry up, Lettice, or you'll have Rundle on your tracks — he'll be back in a minute.'

'I don't want to go,' said Lettice. 'I tell you I feel that nervous — '

'Nonsense, child,' said the cook. 'Run along with you.'

No sooner had the maid gone than Rundle appeared.

'I've had a bit of trouble with Master Antony,' he said. 'He's got it into his head that he wants to come down to dinner. "Rundle," he said to me, confidentially, "do you think it would matter us being seven? I want them to meet my new friend." "What friend, Mr Fairfield?" I said. "Oh," he said, "haven't you seen her? She's always about with me now". Poor chap, he used to be the pick of the bunch, and now I'm afraid he's going potty.'

'Do you really think he'll come down to dinner?' asked the cook, but before Rundle could answer Lettice rushed into the room.

'Oh,' she cried, 'I knew it would be something horrid! I knew it would be! And now she wants a floor cloth and pail! She says they mustn't know anything about it! But I won't go again — I won't bring it down. I won't even touch it.'

'What won't you touch?'

'That waste-paper basket.'

'Why, what's the matter with it?'

'It's . . . it's all bloody!'

When the word was out she grew calmer, and even seemed anxious to relate her experience.

'I went upstairs directly she rang' ('That's an untruth to start with,' said the cook) 'and she opened the door a little way and said, "Oh, Lettice, I've been so scared!" And I said, "What's the matter, miss?" and she said (deceitful-like, as it turned out), "There's a cat in here." Well, I didn't think that was much to be frightened of, so I said, "Shall I come in and catch him, miss?" and she said, "I should be so grateful." Then I went in, but I couldn't see the cat anywhere, so I said, "Where is he?" At which she pointed to the waste-paper basket away by the dressing-table and said, "In that waste-paper basket." I said, "Why, that makes it easier, miss, if he'll stay there." She said, "Oh, he'll stay there all right." Of course I took her meaning in a moment, because I know cats do choose queer, out-of-the-way places to die in, so I said, "You mean the poor creature's dead, miss?" and I was just going across to get him because ordinarily I don't mind the body of an animal, when she said (I will do her that justice), "Stop a minute, Lettice, he isn't dead; he's been murdered." I saw she was all trembling, and that made me tremble too. And when I looked in the basket – well – '

She paused, partly perhaps to enjoy the dramatic effect of her announcement. 'Well, if it wasn't our Thomas! Only you couldn't have recognized him, poor beast, his head was bashed in that cruel.'

'Thomas!' said the cook. 'Why, he was here only an hour ago.'

'That's what I said to Miss Winthrop, "Why, he was in the kitchen only an hour ago," and then I came over funny, and when she asked me to help her clean the mess up I couldn't, not if my life depended on it. But I don't feel like that now,' she ended inconsequently. 'I'll go back and do it!' She collected her traps and departed.

'Thomas!' muttered Rundle. 'Who could have wished the poor beast any harm? Now I remember, Mr Fairfield did ask me to get him out a clean shirt . . . I'd better go up and ask him.'

He found Anthony in evening dress seated at the writing-table. He had stripped it of writing materials and the light from two candles gleamed on its polished surface. Opposite to him on the other side of the table was an empty chair. He was sitting with his back to the room; his face, when he turned it at Rundle's entrance, was blotchy and looked terribly tired.

'I decided to dine here after all, Rundle,' he said. Rundle saw that the Bovril was still untouched in his cup.

'Why, your supper'll get cold, Mr Fairfield,' he said.

'Mind your own business,' said Antony, 'I'm waiting.'

The Empire clock on the drawing-room chimney-piece began to strike, breaking into a conversation which neither at dinner nor afterwards had been more than desultory.

'Eleven,' said Mr Ampleforth. 'The nurse will be here any time now. She ought to be grateful to you, Ronald, for getting him into bed.'

'I didn't enjoy treating Antony like that,' said Ronald. There was a silence.

'What was that?' asked Maggie suddenly.

'It sounded like the motor.'

'Might have been,' said Mr Ampleforth. 'You can't tell from here.'

They strained their ears, but the rushing sound had already died away. 'Eileen's gone to bed, Maggie,' said Mrs Ampleforth. 'Why don't you? We'll wait up for the nurse, and tell you when she comes.'

Rather reluctantly, Maggie agreed to go.

She had been in her bedroom about ten minutes, and was feeling too tired to take her clothes off, when there came a knock at the door. It was Eileen.

'Maggie,' she said, 'the nurse has arrived. I thought you'd like to know.'

'Oh, how kind of you,' said Maggie. 'They were going to tell me, but I expect they forgot. Where is she?'

'In Antony's room. I was coming from the bath and his door was open.'

'Did she look nice?'

'I only saw her back.'

'I think I'll go along and speak to her,' said Maggie.

'Yes, do. I don't think I'll go with you.'

As she walked along the passage, Maggie wondered what she would say to the nurse. She didn't mean to offer her professional advice. But even nurses are human, and Maggie didn't want this stranger to imagine that Antony was, well, always like that – the spoilt, tiresome, unreasonable creature of the last few hours. She could find no harsher epithets for him, even after all his deliberate unkindness. The woman would probably have heard that Maggie was his fiancée; Maggie would try to show her that she was proud of the relationship and felt it an honour.

The door was still open, so she knocked and walked in. But the figure that uncoiled itself from Antony's pillow and darted at her a look of malevolent triumph was not a nurse, nor was her face strange to Maggie; Maggie could see, so intense was her vision at that moment, just what strokes Antony had used to transform her own portrait into Lady Elinor's. She was terrified, but she could not bear to see Antony's rather long hair nearly touching the floor nor the creature's thin hand on his labouring throat. She advanced, resolved at whatever cost to break up this dreadful tableau. She approached near enough to realize that what seemed a stranglehold was probably a caress, when Antony's eyes rolled up at her and words, frothy and toneless like a chain of bursting bubbles, came popping from the corner of his swollen mouth: 'Get out, damn you!' At the same moment she heard the stir of presences behind her and a voice saying, 'Here is the patient, nurse; I'm afraid he's half out of bed, and here's Maggie, too. What *have* you been doing to him, Maggie?' Dazed, she turned about. 'Can't you see?' she cried; but she might have asked the question of herself, for when she looked back she could only see the tumbled bed, the vacant pillow, and Antony's hair trailing the floor.

The nurse was a sensible woman. Fortified by tea, she soon bundled everybody out of the room. A deeper quiet than night ordinarily brings invaded the house. The reign of illness had begun.

A special embargo was laid on Maggie's visits. The nurse said she had noticed that Miss Winthrop's presence agitated the patient. But Maggie extracted a promise that she should be called if Antony got worse. She was too tired and worried to sleep, even if she had tried to, so she sat up fully dressed in a chair, every now and then trying to allay her anxiety by furtive visits to Antony's bedroom door.

The hours passed on leaden feet. She tried to distract herself by reading the light literature with which her hostess had provided her. Though she could not keep her attention on the books, she continued to turn their pages, for only so could she keep at bay the conviction that had long been forming at the back of her mind and that now threatened to engulf her whole consciousness: the conviction that the legend about Low Threshold was true. She was neither hysterical nor superstitious, and for a moment she had managed to persuade herself that what she had seen in Antony's room was an hallucination. The passing hours robbed her of that solace. Antony was the victim of Lady Elinor's vengeance. Everything pointed to it; the circumstances of her appearance, the nature of Antony's illness, the horrible deterioration in his character – to say nothing of the drawings, and the cat.

There were only two ways of saving him. One was to get him out of the house; she had tried that and failed; if she tried again she would fail more signally than before. But there remained the other way.

The old book about 'The Tragicall Happenings at Low Threshold Hall' still reposed in a drawer; for the sake of her peace of mind Maggie had vowed not to take it out, and till now she had kept her vow. But as the sky began to pale with the promise of dawn and her conviction of Antony's mortal danger grew apace, her resolution broke down.

'Whereby we must conclude,' she read, 'that the Lady Elinor like other Apparitions, is subject to certain Lawes. One, to abandon her Victim and seeking another tenement enter into it and transfer her vengeance, should its path be crossed by a Body yet nearer Dissolution . . .'

A knock, that had been twice repeated, startled her out of her reverie.

'Come in!'

'Miss Winthrop,' said the nurse, 'I'm sorry to tell you the patient is weaker. I think the doctor had better be telephoned for.'

'I'll go and get someone,' said Maggie. 'Is he much worse?'

'Very much, I'm afraid.'

Maggie had no difficulty in finding Rundle; he was already up.

'What time is it, Rundle?' she asked. 'I've lost count.'

'Half-past four, miss.' He looked very sorry for her.

'When will the doctor be here?'

'In about an hour, miss, not more.'

Suddenly she had an idea. 'I'm so tired, Rundle, I think I shall try to get some sleep. Tell them not to call me unless . . . unless . . .'

'Yes, miss,' said Rundle. 'You look altogether done up.'

About an hour! So she had plenty of time. She took up the book again '. . . transfer her vengeance . . . seeking another tenement . . . a Body nearer Dissolution . . .' Her idle thoughts turned with compassion to the poor servant girl whose death had spelt recovery to Lord Deadham's cousin but had been so little regarded: 'the night was spent' before they heard that she was dead. Well, this night was spent already. Maggie shivered. 'I shall die in my sleep,' she thought. 'But shall I feel her come?' Her tired body sickened with nausea at the idea of such a loathsome violation. But the thought still nagged at her. 'Shall I realize even for a moment that I'm changing into . . . into?' Her mind refused to frame the possibility. 'Should I have time to do anyone an injury?' she wondered. 'I could tie my feet together with a handkerchief; that would prevent me from walking.' Walking . . . walking . . . The word let loose on her mind a new flood of terrors. She could not do it! She could not lay herself open for ever to this horrible contemplation! Her tormented imagination began to busy itself with the details of her funeral; she saw mourners following her coffin into the church. But Antony was not amongst them; he was better, but too ill to be there. He could not understand why she had killed herself, for the note she had left gave no hint of the real reason, referred only to continual sleeplessness and nervous depression. So she would not have his company when her body was committed to the ground. But that was a mistake; it would not be her body, it would belong to that other woman and be hers to return to by the right of possession.

All at once the screen which had recorded such vivid images to her mind's eye went blank; and her physical eye, released, roamed wildly about the room. It rested on the book she was still holding. 'She cannot possess or haunt the corpse,' she read, 'after it hath received Christian Buriall.' Here was a ray of comfort. But (her fears warned her) being a suicide she might not be allowed Christian burial. How then? Instead of the churchyard she saw a cross-roads, with a slanting signpost on which the words could no longer be read; only two or three people were there; they kept looking furtively about them, and the grave-digger had thrown his spade aside and was holding a stake . . .

She pulled herself together with a jerk. 'These are all fancies,' she thought. 'It wasn't fancy when I signed the poison book.' She took up the little glass cylinder; there were eighteen tablets and the dose was one or two. Daylight was broadening apace; she must hurry. She took some notepaper and wrote for five minutes. She had reached the words 'No one is to blame' when suddenly her ears were assailed by a tremendous tearing, whirring sound; it grew louder and louder until the whole room vibrated. In the midst of the deafening din something flashed past the window, for a fraction of a second blotting out the daylight. Then there was a crash such as she had never heard in her life.

All else forgotten, Maggie ran to the window. An indescribable scene of wreckage met her eyes. The aeroplane had been travelling at a terrific pace; it was smashed to atoms. To right and left the lawn was littered with fragments, some of which had made great gashes in the grass, exposing the earth. The pilot had been flung clear, she could just see his legs sticking out from a flower-bed under the wall of the house. They did not move and she thought he must be dead.

While she was wondering what to do she heard voices underneath the window.

'We don't seem to be very lucky here just now, Rundle,' said Mr Ampleforth.

'No, sir.'

There was a pause. Then Mr Ampleforth spoke again.

'He's still breathing, I think.'

'Yes, sir, he is, just.'

'You take his head and I'll take his feet, and we'll get him into the house.'

Something began to stir in Maggie's mind. Rundle replied:

'If you'll pardon me saying so, sir, I don't think we ought to move him. I was told once by a doctor that if a man's had a fall or anything it's best to leave him lying.'

'I don't think it'll matter if we're careful.'

'Really, sir, if you'll take my advice – '

There was a note of obstinacy in Rundle's voice. Maggie, almost beside herself with agitation, longed to fling open the window and cry, 'Bring him in! Bring him in!' But her hand seemed paralysed and her throat could not form the words.

Presently Mr Ampleforth said:

'You know, we can't let him stay here. It's beginning to rain.'

(Bring him in! Bring him in!)

'Well, sir, it's your responsibility . . .'

Maggie's heart almost stopped beating.

'Naturally I don't want to do anything to hurt the poor chap.'

(Oh, bring him in! Bring him in!)

The rain began to patter on the pane.

'Look here, Rundle, we must get him under cover.'

'I'll fetch that bit of wing, sir, and put it over him.'

(Bring him in! Bring him in!)

Maggie heard Rundle pulling something that grated on the gravel path. The sound ceased and Mr Ampleforth said:

'The very thing for a stretcher, Rundle! The earth's so soft we can slide it under him. Careful, careful!' Both men were breathing hard. 'Have you got your end? Right.' Their heavy, measured footfalls grew fainter and fainter.

The next thing Maggie heard was the car returning with the doctor. Not daring to go out and unable to sit down, she stood, how long she did not know, holding her bedroom door ajar.

At last she saw the nurse coming towards her.

'The patient's a little better, Miss Winthrop. The doctor thinks he'll pull through now.'

'Which patient?'

'Oh, there was never any hope for the other poor fellow.'

Maggie closed her eyes.

'Can I see Antony?' she said at last.

'Well, you may just peep at him.'

Antony smiled at her feebly from the bed.

# August Heat

W. F. HARVEY

PENISTONE ROAD, CLAPHAM,
*August 20th, 190—*

I have had what I believe to be the most remarkable day in my life, and while the events are still fresh in my mind, I wish to put them down on paper as clearly as possible.

Let me say at the outset that my name is James Clarence Withencroft.

I am forty years old, in perfect health, never having known a day's illness.

By profession I am an artist, not a very successful one, but I earn enough money by my black-and-white work to satisfy my necessary wants.

My only relative, a sister, died five years ago, so that I am independent.

I breakfasted this morning at nine, and after glancing through the morning paper I lighted my pipe and proceeded to let my mind wander in the hope that I might chance upon some subject for my pencil.

The room, though door and windows were open, was oppressively hot, and I had just made up my mind that the coolest and most comfortable place in the neighbourhood would be the deep end of the public swimming bath, when the idea came.

I began to draw. So intent was I on my work that I left my lunch untouched, only stopping work when the clock of St Jude's struck four.

The final result, for a hurried sketch, was, I felt sure, the best thing I had done.

It showed a criminal in the dock immediately after the judge had pronounced sentence. The man was fat — enormously fat. The flesh hung in rolls about his chin; it creased his huge stumpy neck. He was clean shaven (perhaps I should say a few days before he must have been clean shaven) and almost bald. He stood in the dock, his short, clumsy fingers clasping the rail, looking straight in front of him. The feeling that his expression conveyed was not so much one of horror as of utter absolute collapse.

There seemed nothing in the man strong enough to sustain that mountain of flesh.

I rolled up the sketch, and without quite knowing why, placed it in my pocket. Then with the rare sense of happiness which the knowledge of a good thing well done gives, I left the house.

I believe that I set out with the idea of calling upon Trenton, for I remember walking along Lytton Street and turning to the right along Gilchrist Road at the bottom of the hill where the men were at work on the new tram lines.

From there onwards I have only the vaguest recollection of where I went. The one thing of which I was fully conscious was the awful heat, that came up from the dusty asphalt pavement as an almost palpable wave. I longed for the thunder promised by the great banks of copper-coloured cloud that hung low over the western sky.

I must have walked five or six miles, when a small boy roused me from my reverie by asking the time.

It was twenty minutes to seven.

When he left me I began to take stock of my bearings. I found myself standing before a gate that led into a yard bordered by a strip of thirsty earth, where there were flowers, purple stock and scarlet geranium. Above the entrance was a board with the inscription —

CHS. ATKINSON.　　　MONUMENTAL MASON.
WORKER IN ENGLISH AND ITALIAN MARBLES

From the yard itself came a cheery whistle, the noise of hammer blows, and the cold sound of steel meeting stone.

A sudden impulse made me enter.

A man was sitting with his back towards me, busy at work on a slab of curiously veined marble. He turned round as he heard my steps and I stopped short.

It was the man I had been drawing, whose portrait lay in my pocket.

He sat there, huge and elephantine, the sweat pouring from his scalp, which he wiped with a red silk handkerchief. But though the face was the same, the expression was absolutely different.

He greeted me smiling, as if we were old friends, and shook my hand.

I apologized for my intrusion.

'Everything is hot and glary outside,' I said. 'This seems an oasis in the wilderness.'

'I don't know about the oasis,' he replied, 'but it certainly is hot, as hot as hell. Take a seat, sir!'

He pointed to the end of the gravestone on which he was at work, and I sat down.

'That's a beautiful piece of stone you've got hold of,' I said.

He shook his head. 'In a way it is,' he answered, 'the surface here is as fine as anything you could wish, but there's a big flaw at the back, though I don't expect you'd ever notice it. I could never make a really good job of a bit of marble like that. It would be all right in a summer like this; it wouldn't mind the blasted heat. But wait till the winter comes. There's nothing quite like frost to find out the weak points in stone.'

'Then what's it for?' I said.

The man burst out laughing.

'You'd hardly believe me if I was to tell you it's for an exhibition, but it's the truth. Artists have exhibitions: so do grocers and butchers; we have them too. All the latest little things in headstones, you know.'

He went on to talk of marbles, which sort best withstood wind and rain, and which were easiest to work; then of his garden and a new sort of carnation he had bought. At the end of every other minute he would drop his tools, wipe his shining head, and curse the heat.

I said little, for I felt uneasy. There was something

unnatural, uncanny, in meeting this man.

I tried to persuade myself that I had seen him before, that his face, unknown to me, had found a place in some out-of-the-way corner of my memory, but I knew that I was practising little more than a plausible piece of self-deception.

Mr Atkinson finished his work, spat on the ground, and got up with a sigh of relief.

'There! What do you think of that?' he said with an air of evident pride.

The inscription which I read for the first time was this:

SACRED TO THE MEMORY
OF
JAMES CLARENCE WITHENCROFT
BORN JAN. 18TH, 1860
HE PASSED AWAY VERY SUDDENLY
ON AUGUST 20TH, 190—
*'In the midst of life we are in death'*

For some time I sat in silence. Then a cold shudder ran down my spine. I asked him where he had seen the name.

'Oh, I didn't see it anywhere,' replied Mr Atkinson, 'I wanted some name, and I put down the first that came into my head. Why do you want to know?'

'It's a strange coincidence, but it happens to be mine.'

He gave a long, low whistle.

'And the dates?'

'I can only answer for one of them and that's correct.'

'It's a rum go!' he said.

But he knew less than I did. I told him of my morning's work. I took the sketch from my pocket and showed it to him. As he looked, the expression on his face altered until it became more and more like that of the man I had drawn.

'And it was only the day before yesterday,' he said, 'that I told Maria there were no such things as ghosts!'

Neither of us had seen a ghost, but I knew what he meant.

'You probably heard my name,' I said.

'And you must have seen me somewhere and have forgotten it! Were you at Clacton-on-Sea last July?'

I had never been to Clacton in my life. We were silent for some time. We were both looking at the same thing, the two dates on the gravestone, and one was right.

'Come inside and have some supper,' said Mr Atkinson.

His wife is a cheerful little woman, with the flaky red cheeks of the country-bred. Her husband introduced me as a friend of his who was an artist. The result was unfortunate, for after the sardines and watercress had been removed, she brought out a Doré Bible and I had to sit and express my admiration for nearly an hour.

I went outside, and found Atkinson sitting on the gravestone, smoking.

We resumed the conversation at the point we had left off.

'You must excuse me asking,' I said, 'but do you know of anything you've done for which you could be put on trial?'

He shook his head.

'I'm not a bankrupt, the business is prosperous enough. Three years ago I gave turkeys to some of the guardians at Christmas, but that's all I can think of. And they were small ones, too,' he added as an afterthought.

He got up, fetched a can from the porch, and began

to water the flowers. 'Twice a day regular in the hot weather,' he said, 'and then the heat sometimes gets the better of the delicate ones. And ferns, good Lord! They could never stand it. Where do you live?'

I told him my address. It would take an hour's quick walk to get back home.

'It's like this,' he said. 'We'll look at the matter straight. If you go back home tonight, you take your chance of accidents. A cart may run over you, and there's always banana skins and orange peel, to say nothing of falling ladders.'

He spoke of the improbable with an intense seriousness that would have been laughable six hours before. But I did not laugh.

'The best thing we can do,' he continued, 'is for you to stay here till twelve o'clock. We'll go upstairs and smoke, it may be cooler inside.'

To my surprise I agreed.

We are sitting now in a long, low room beneath the eaves. Atkinson has sent his wife to bed. He himself is busy sharpening some tools at a little oilstone, smoking one of my cigars the while.

The air seems charged with thunder. I am writing this at a shaky table before the open window. The leg is cracked, and Atkinson, who seems a handy man with his tools, is going to mend it as soon as he has finished putting an edge on his chisel.

It is after eleven now. I shall be gone in less than an hour.

But the heat is stifling.

It is enough to send a man mad.

# The Return of the Native

WILLIAM CROFT DICKINSON

'The trouble with all you Scots is that you live too much in the past.'

Galbraith was trailing his coat as usual, but this time it was MacDonald, our visiting Fulbright Professor, who took up the challenge.

'The trouble is that sometimes we cannot escape the past,' he said.

'None of us can,' retorted Galbraith. 'The past in the present is obvious all the time.'

'I meant something a little different from that,' replied MacDonald. 'I meant a past that may come back, unexpectedly, to disturb the present.'

For once Galbraith seemed to be at a loss. 'In what way?' he asked, lamely.

'Well,' answered MacDonald, 'I could give you one instance from my own experience. if you'd care for it. It's a story I don't often tell, and I can't say that I emerged with credit; but it certainly underlines the point I wanted to make.'

Our American guest looked at us a little shyly, as though wondering whether he had broken one of the rules of the Common Room in offering to recount a 'personal experience'. He was quickly reassured: and this was his story of a past which could not be escaped.

About a year after the end of World War II, when I was still an officer in the American Intelligence, and stationed in London, I decided to seize the opportunity of visiting Scotland and seeing, for the first time, the land of my folk. I had little difficulty in obtaining a fortnight's leave and, after spending a week-end in Edinburgh, I hired a small car to drive to Arisaig and Morar — the district from which I knew my forbears had emigrated some two hundred years ago.

Setting off from Edinburgh on the Monday morning, I made that marvellous drive through Callander, Loch-earnhead, and Tyndrum, and on through Glencoe to Ballachulish, where I put up for the night. Passing through Balquhidder country on my way from Callander to Tyndrum, I had recalled the story of assembled Macgregors swearing their oaths on the severed head of a royal forester; and, as I had passed through Glencoe, I recalled the tragedy of sleeping MacDonalds who were massacred by those to whom they had given food and shelter. Yet that night, in the inn at Ballachulish, as I brooded over the stories of the past, I little thought that I myself was soon to be touched by the past — touched too closely for my liking — and simply because I, too, was a MacDonald, though a MacDonald of a different sept from the MacIans of Glencoe.

The Tuesday morning broke fine and clear. Leaving Ballachulish, I crossed by the ferry and took the lovely road by the shores of Loch Linnhe and Loch Eil, and on to Glenfinnan, where Prince Charlie's standard was raised, and where I thought the monument a poor thing to commemorate so stirring an event. From Glenfinnan the scenery became more wonderful still, as the narrow road, still 'unimproved', twisted and turned on its ledge between the hills and the sea: and I remembered I was on 'The Road to the Isles'.

It may be that my head was too full of the tales of the Young Chevalier, or it may be that my eyes strayed too often to the beauty of land and sea: I do not know. But, almost too late, I caught sight of an enormous boulder crashing down the hillside and almost on top of my car. Braking hard, and wrenching the wheel violently to the right, I lost control of the car and ran into the bank of the hill, while the boulder, missing the front of the car by inches, thundered across the road and bounded over the opposite verge.

Slightly shaken, I got out to see what damage I had done, and, as I did so, I was astonished to see an old woman standing on the other side of the road just where the boulder had crashed across. For a moment I wondered how she had escaped; then, something in her appearance made me look at her more closely. I was startled to see that her dark and deep-set eyes were glaring at me with a look of intense hate. I saw, too, that water was dripping from her clothes and that her grey hair was hanging round her shoulders, dank and wet. And, looking at her, I experienced a strange sense of danger, or it might even have been fear, which it is wholly impossible to describe.

So we stood, facing one another, and myself in a kind of trance, until, suddenly, the woman turned away and, apparently stepping down from the road, disappeared over the edge. Recovering my wits, I ran across the road, only to pull myself up with a jerk. On that side of the road, and guarded only by a single strand of wire, there was a sheer drop of a hundred feet or more to the rocks on the loch-side below. Had I wrenched my wheel the other way, or had that boulder crashed into my small car, broadside on, nothing could have saved me.

I made myself look again at that sheer drop. What had happened to the old woman? There was no sign of her anywhere. Not even a ghastly huddle of body and clothes on the rocks below. Yet I had seen her clearly enough, and she had stepped down from the road at this very spot. And why had she glared at me with such bitter hate? Surely I had not fallen asleep at the wheel and dreamed the whole thing – a boulder crashing down and a malevolent old hag with dripping clothes?

I walked slowly back to the car, trying to puzzle things out. Fortunately the car was not badly damaged: a buckled wing and little more. But it was firmly wedged in the bank and would not move. I sat down beside it and waited for help. And help soon came in the shape of a delivery van; its driver fortunately had a length of rope; and within a few minutes he had hauled me clear.

'You were lucky in your skid,' he said, cheerfully. 'Had you skidded the other way you'd have finished driving for good. And it would have been pretty difficult to recover your remains for the funeral. However, all's well now. And that front wheel seems all right, too. But it's queer the way you managed to skid on a dry surface like this.'

'I didn't skid,' I replied, slowly. 'I was trying to avoid a boulder that was rolling down the hillside on to the road.'

'Boulder!' he answered, looking me hard in the eye. 'It's the first time I've heard of a boulder rolling down on to this road. And I've driven over it six days a week for the last twelve years or so.' Then, still looking me straight in the eye, he wavered a little and condescended to add: 'However, strange things do happen. But I'd like to know where that boulder came from. So long.'

He waved a friendly hand, got into his van, and drove off, leaving me alone with uncomfortable thoughts. I was positive I had not fallen asleep. I was equally positive that a large boulder had missed my car by inches. And what of that old woman with her dank hair and dripping clothes, who might almost have arisen from the waters of the loch below and who, after glaring at me with burning hate, had apparently been swallowed up in the waters again? If not, where had she gone? And who was she, anyway? How did she fit in? 'Well,' I said to myself, resignedly, 'strange things certainly do happen. But I'd be glad of an explanation, if anyone could give it.'

I stepped into my car, started the engine, and drove on again. Possibly I was more shaken than I had at first realized, and possibly I was worried with my thoughts; certainly I now crawled along the road, through Arisaig, and on to Morar. I remember that when at last I pulled into the drive of my hotel I felt as though a great burden had suddenly been lifted from my back.

Morar is a lovely spot, with its stretch of silver sand and with the islands of Rum, Eigg and Muck standing like sentinels in the sea. Inland, I found delightful walks, especially one by the side of the loch. In a couple of days the old woman of my adventure on the road from Glenfinnan had become a puzzling memory, and nothing more.

I had reached Morar on the Tuesday evening. Wednesday and Thursday I spent in lazily wandering about, or in lying in the heather and feeling how good, for a time, was a life of ease. On Friday, much against my inclination, I caught up with some long-delayed mail from home and then, in the early evening, took a short walk that led to the falls, where the waters of the loch, at that time still unharnessed for electric power, poured through a gorge before finding their way to the sea.

I had scrambled down a steep and narrow path that led to the foot of the falls, and had taken my stance on a boulder there, when a noise, rising above the thunder of the falls, made me turn round. I was only half-interested, and I turned round casually, but, to my horror, I saw a large rock hurtling down the narrow path on which I stood. How I managed to make the right decision in a split second of time, I shall never know. I flung myself down behind the boulder on which I was standing. The rock struck it with a mighty crack, bounced harmlessly over my head, and plunged down into the whirlpool at the bottom of the falls.

Dazed and trembling, I carefully picked myself up. Then pain made itself felt, and I discovered that I had injured my left knee by throwing myself down to the ground. Would I be able to climb back again to the top of the path? I looked up at that steep and broken slope, and my heart suddenly jumped into my throat. An old woman with dank grey hair, and with clothes that were dripping wet, was glaring at me from above; glaring at me with intense hate, as three days before she had glared at me on the road from Glenfinnan. And again, though this time far more pronounced, I felt the same strange fear, and, with it, a weakness that seemed to affect every part of me.

I gripped the boulder beside me with both hands, frightened lest I should fall backwards into the whirl-pool below. Gradually the weakness passed. Then, summoning the little courage that was left in me, I began a slow and painful crawl on hands and knees, taking advantage of every turn in the path, and praying constantly that no other rock would be hurled against me from above. When, at long last, I reached the top of the path, I lay there completely exhausted and unable to take a further step. The old woman was nowhere to be seen.

As I lay there, worn out and riddled with fear, my mind strove vainly to grapple with accidents that were beyond all reasoning. I now knew definitely that I had not fallen asleep at the wheel of my car. I knew, too, that twice a fiend of an old woman had tried to send me to the shades from which I was convinced she her-

self had risen. I had had enough. If, all unwittingly, I
had disturbed the haunts of some avenging 'ghost', the
only answer was to leave her haunts forthwith. Call me
a coward, if you like; and coward I certainly became!
But, then and there, I determined to return to Edinburgh and the safety of its streets.

I limped slowly back to the hotel, intending to pack
my bags and depart. Yet, as soon as I had reached the
hotel, a new fear struck me. To leave forthwith would
mean driving through Arisaig, and on to Glenfinnan,
by night. I couldn't face it. I knew that even driving
along that road by day I should be crawling at a snail's
pace, and looking to the right and left of me all the
time. I even had thoughts of driving the odd four miles
into Mallaig and there putting myself and my car on
the boat. In the end I decided to stay the night, and to
leave on the Saturday morning.


After dinner I told the landlord of my decision to leave
early the next morning. I excused myself by reference
to some urgent business that had arisen from my mail;
and, in expressing my appreciation of the comfort of
my stay, murmured something of my regret at having
to leave so soon, and before I had even made any
attempt to trace my ancestors who had come from
Morar about two hundred years ago.

'Have you seen Father MacWilliam?' came his unex-
pected reply.

'No,' I answered. 'Why do you ask?'

'Well, it will be this way,' he said. 'The Father knows
the history of Morar. He's been at the books and the
papers these many years. And he's the one who would
be telling you about your own folks, way past, if,
indeed, there is anything to be known of them at all.'

'Could I call upon him now?' I asked eagerly.

'Indeed you could; but he'd be out.'

I looked at him in surprise.

'He'd be out, for he's in my own parlour this very time. Come you with me, and you can have a talk with him before you go.'

Full of interest, I was led to the back-parlour of the hotel, where Father MacWilliam, a plump and rosy-faced priest, was snugly ensconced in an easy-chair, and deep in the pages of an enormous book.

'Father, I've brought you Mr John MacDonald,' said my host, without further ado. 'He's for leaving tomorrow, but he'd be glad if you could be telling him of his people who, it would seem, came from these parts maybe two hundred years ago. If I were to let the two of you talk together, maybe he'll be learning something of what he wants to know.'

The priest gave me a warm smile of welcome, and somehow managed to unfold himself out of his chair. The landlord gave us a nod, and left the two of us together.

'John MacDonald,' said the priest, looking at me. 'It tells me nothing. Everyone here is a MacDonald. Every man, woman and child. God bless them all. Could you tell me more?'

I had to confess that I couldn't. All I knew was that my forbears had left Morar, or some place in its vicinity, about the 1750s. That, and no more.

Father MacWilliam shook his head. ' 'Tis no use,' he said. 'I can be of no help to you, much as I would have liked. Too many MacDonalds have left these parts – and sometimes I think too many have stayed on. But there, you've had a good time for the few days you've been here. And that's aye something.'

'Yes,' I answered slowly, and then, with a sudden desire to unburden myself, 'a good enough time if it hadn't been for an old woman who has twice tried to stone me to death '

'What?' shouted the priest, his eyes suddenly blazing. 'You will be telling me that! Were her clothes dripping with water? Did you see, man, did you see?'

'Yes,' I answered, quickly. 'They were dripping wet. And she glared at me with such hatred in her eyes that I knew she was trying to kill me. Who is she? Or what is she?'

'I know only too well what she is,' he replied, slowly and quietly. 'And I know now who you are, John MacDonald, and I can give you your forbears. I'm thinking, 'tis well you'll be leaving when the morning comes. But tell me your tale, and I'll tell you mine.'

Briefly I told him of my two encounters – on the road from Glenfinnan, and on the path by the falls. I told him, too, of the feeling of fear that had come to me. 'But why,' I protested, 'why should this old hag – ghost or spirit or fiend or whatever she is – hate me, a complete stranger, and try to murder me?'

'Because you are no stranger,' answered the priest, gravely. 'You are a MacDonald of Grianan, and the curse is on you and all your kin. That's why. And there's more to it. The same curse made your own people sell all, pack up, and sail across the seas in the year 1754. And though I'd be the last man to be frightening you, I shall be glad when you're back in your own land again.'

'But the thing's impossible,' I burst out, even though my own experiences had told me the very contrary.

'Not at all,' he replied firmly. 'Doesn't the Holy Book itself speak of evil and foul spirits? And didn't an evil spirit attack the seven sons of Sceva, leaping upon them, and driving them away, wounded and naked?'

'Well, what is the curse?' I demanded impatiently.

'That the stones of the earth shall crush you and all your kin,' answered the priest, looking at me sadly. 'And I'd be glad to be seeing you escape.'

'But why should there be such a curse?' I pleaded.

'Listen, my son. Away back in the seventeenth century the MacDonalds of Grianan were big folk, holding their land by charter of the king and with a right of judging the people on their land – even with a right of *furca et fossa*, a right of "gallows and pit", a gallows for hanging guilty men, and a pit for drowning guilty women. And in that time, when many a poor woman was put to death because she was reputed to be a witch, Angus MacDonald of Grianan, you'll forgive me, was a cruel man. Then it was that Isabel Mackenzie, a poor creature on his lands, was accused of witchcraft because a neighbour's cow had sickened and died. Isabel Mackenzie was condemned to death, and Angus MacDonald, the cruel man, decreed it should be death by drowning. Did not his own charter say so? That poor creature was tied by her wrists to the length of a rope; the rope was tied to a boat; and Angus himself, with others of his house, rowed out into the loch, dragging her behind them till at last she was drowned.

'Then, it is said, as the waters slowly ended her unhappy life, she cursed Angus and all his kin. "The waters of the loch shall drown me, but the stones of the earth shall crush you and all your kin – *Pronnaidh clachan na talmhainn thu 's do chinneadh uile.*" '

The priest paused. 'And so it has been,' he continued, with a sigh. 'Angus laughed, as the years passed and he still lived. But one night, in a storm of wind, the chimney of his house was blown down and the stones of it fell through the roof and crushed him to death where he lay in his bed.

'Alastair, his son, was of finer mould. I can find no word of him doing wrong to man or beast. Yet he, too, was to die. There was a jetty to be built – and this was maybe a full twenty years after his father had died – and Alastair had gone down to see the men at the work. There was a tackle of some kind for lifting the heavy stones, and, somehow, a stone slipped from the tackle. It fell on him and crushed him to death.

'Then it was that people began to look at Grianan and quietly, among themselves, began to talk of the curse. And then it was that the MacDonalds of Grianan began to die more quickly. Always there was a stone of the earth in the way of their dying; and some of them, with their last words, would be speaking strange things – of a woman with burning eyes, and whose clothes were wet with the waters of the loch. And, in the end, one Roderick MacDonald, having seen his own father crushed to death by a millstone that was firmly fixed and yet somehow broke loose, sold his lands and his cattle, and sailed to America with his wife and child.

'And you, my son,' said Father MacWilliam, laying his hand gently on my arm, 'you are come of Roderick's stock. Yet I see some comfort for you. In all the papers that I have read, Isabel Mackenzie's curse never failed before. Twice it has failed to touch you. To me it would seem that her evil power is on the wane. I shall pray for you. But I shall still be glad to see you gone.'

'And I can do nothing?' I asked lamely.

'Nothing, save to put your trust in God,' he answered. 'And to remember that the power of the Lord is greater than all the powers of evil.'

Again he touched me lightly on the arm, looked kindly at me, and went out.

To be quite frank, I do not remember very clearly how I passed the rest of that evening. I was already completely unnerved, and now the story of my own house, the house that had the curse upon it, occupied my mind to the exclusion of all else. I wanted company. I wanted to have people around me. And yet my mind was never on the talk that they made. I am ashamed to think how boorish and uncivil I must have seemed. I am ashamed, too, to think of the drink that I took. I freely admit that terror had taken hold of me. Terror of being left alone. Terror of going to my bed. I drank in the bar, trying to make friends with complete strangers and yet thinking always of an old woman and her curse on my kin. In the end, I am told, I had to be carried to bed by the local doctor and a guest at the hotel. For a time, drink had ousted terror.

I do not know what time it was when I awoke. It was already daylight – but daylight breaks early in the Highlands in summer time. My head ached violently. Then I remembered my heavy drinking, and, with that, I remembered its cause. But what had awakened me? The wind was blowing strongly and yet, I assured myself, not strongly enough to bring a chimney-stack crashing down. But what was that? My ears caught a strange noise that seemed to come from the corridor outside my room. At once all my terror returned. I sat up in bed. There was the noise again! A shuffling noise. And something more. A noise that came between each shuffle. What was it? A shuffle; a strange dull thump; a shuffle; a thump. And drawing nearer all the time.

I tried to shout, but I could only croak like a feeble frog. I jumped out of bed, trembling from head to foot. How could I escape? Outside, in the corridor, a hell-hag, dead three hundred years ago, was coming to me, coming to crush me to death with a stone. A stone! That was the noise I could hear! She was pushing it before her, pushing it up to my door!

I looked wildly round. Thank God! The window! Flinging it wide open, I climbed quickly out, and, hanging from the window-ledge by my hands, let myself drop. As I landed on the ground I fell over backwards, and, at the same instant, there came a heavy thud at my feet and the soft garden-earth splashed over me. I lay there, paralysed with fear.

Then, slowly, I raised my head to look. A large stone had embedded itself in the ground exactly where I had dropped and exactly where I would have been had I not fallen over on my back. The curse was still upon me, and my life was to end with a stone.

I sprang to my feet, and, strangely, found my voice again. With a wild cry I ran across the garden, my injured knee sending quivers of hot pain up my thigh. And immediately I was held in a fast grip. Trembling and overwrought, I whimpered like a beaten cur, only to be at once calmed and reassured. I had run straight into the arms of Father MacWilliam.

'You are safe, my son,' came his gentle voice, as he still held me in his arms. 'Safe and saved. The powers of darkness shall trouble you no more. I have wrestled, even as Jacob wrestled at Peniel. Come with me to my own house. The Lord forgive me: I should have taken you there before.'

Paying no attention to the confused hubbub that now came from the hotel, he led me gently across the road – its stones feeling smooth and cool to my bare feet – and over the open moorland to the church. There he took me into his house and put me in his own bed. On the instant, I fell into peaceful sleep.

Late the next morning I awoke to find my clothes on a chair by my bed. I washed and dressed, and went downstairs. A wise and gentle priest was awaiting me. He gave me breakfast, and then took me to my car which, with all my luggage packed and neatly stowed on the rear seat, was standing at his gate. 'There you are, my son,' he said. 'The curse is at an end. You can take any road and drive on it as freely as you wish – though,' he added, with a twinkle in his eye, 'always observing the laws that are enforced by the police.' He gave me his blessing, and wished me God-speed. With unashamed tears in my eyes, I thanked him again and again. At last I drove away.

Without a qualm, without fear of any kind, I drove back through Arisaig and Glenfinnan, back through Ballachulish and Callander, and so to Edinburgh.

Yet my tale has not quite ended.

On my way back, I stopped at Ballachulish for a very late lunch at the inn. As I ate alone in the dining-room, I heard two men talking outside by the open window.

'That was a mighty queer business last night, though I could get nothing out of the landlord when I tried to pump him this morning.'

'Yes, but the fellow was obviously drunk. He had to be carried to bed, you know.'

'I agree, old man. All the same, there was more to it than that. As you know, my room was next to his, and, just before he gave that awful yell which woke up everybody, I'd already been wakened by a strange kind of bumping noise which I couldn't fathom. I got up and looked out of the window, thinking the noise was probably coming from outside – and it may well have been that coping-stone, which had obviously worked loose, and which the wind may have been lifting slightly before it fell.

'However, that's not what I was going to say. As I looked out of the window, there, in the clear light of the early morning, I was astonished to see the local priest standing in the middle of the lawn, with one arm raised above his head, while a dishevelled old woman crouched and cowered before him. The very next second I saw this fellow climb out of his window and drop down. There was a crash as the coping-stone fell. And, with that, he jumped up, gave his appalling yell, and rushed straight into the arms of the priest. Where the old woman had gone to I don't know. She just seemed to disappear. And what she and the priest were doing . . .'

'What an extraordinary . . . Did you . . .'

The men had moved away, and their voices were fading. I tiptoed as fast as I could to the window and strained my ears. But I could catch only a few more words.

'And another queer thing – when I dashed out into the corridor in my bare feet it seemed to be soaking wet all along its length.'

# Coincidence

A. J. ALAN

This is the story of a coincidence. At any rate I call it a coincidence.

The road where I live is very long and very straight. It's paved with wood and well lighted after dark. The result is that cars and taxis going by during the night . . . often go quite fast. I don't blame 'em. They hardly ever wake me unless they stop near the house.

However, about two months ago one did.

I mean he did wake me. He jammed on his brakes for all he was worth just opposite my window and pulled up dead. You know what a row that makes. Then after quite a short pause he drove on again. That was nothing, of course, and it didn't make much impression on me at the moment. I was only just not asleep. But about two minutes later the same thing happened again. This time it was a taxi – at least it sounded like a taxi. Just about the same place the driver shoved on his brakes with a regular scream and *he* stopped. Then I think he backed a few yards, but I don't know. At all events he did a bit of shunting and in a minute or two *he* cleared off. As you can imagine this second . . . business . . . made more of an impression, and when still a third car went through the same . . . programme – I really did quite try to address my mind to the problem. You know how utterly vague one can be at three o'clock in the morning. I said, 'Oh, yes. I know what it is – it's the same as last February.'

In February, or was it January? – anyway whenever it was – the water main bust – and a hole became in the middle of the road. They fenced it off with poles and red lamps, and put a watchman and brazier and sentry box inside.

That was all right, of course, but during the night a thickish fog came on, and cars came whizzing along, banking on a clear road, and didn't see the lights until they were nearly on top of them, and had to pull up in a hurry. Can't you see the watchman striking out for the shore – after the first two or three? mit brazier.

At all events I thought, 'That's what's happened again.' But then I said, 'Hang it all it's *August* – there can't be a fog – so it isn't that. This must be looked into.' So I got out of bed and went and hung out of the window. Presently a large touring car came buzzing along and just opposite me on went the brakes and it tried to loop the loop like the others had. I couldn't quite see where it had pulled up because there are rather a lot of trees on each side of my window, but I heard people get out and there was a general air of excitement for about a minute. Then they climbed in again and the door banged and away they went. You can quite imagine how intriguing it all was. I said, 'This cannot be borne for another moment. I simply must go and see what it's all about.' So I put on some slippers and my dressing gown (pale blue, and much admired about the house) and went downstairs and out ino the road.

Beautiful warm night and no end of a moon. I looked up and down but there wasn't a thing in sight, and apparently nothing whatever wrong with the road. So I crossed over to where the marks of skidding began. There were great shining scrawks all over the shop – and then I saw the cause of all the trouble. The moonlight was pretty bright, and about fifteen yards up the road was a patch of deep shadow thrown by a tree. In this shadow there was a man lying. His back was towards me and his feet were about a yard from the pavement. He seemed to be dressed in light brown clothes – not exactly a check pattern but ruled off in squares, so to speak. You often see girls with cloaks made of that kind of stuff.

Well, of course, I started walking up the road towards him, but when I got within five or six yards an extraordinary thing happened. He disappeared. At least he didn't exactly disappear, but I suddenly saw what he really was. He was a rough patch in the road – er . . . don't misjudge me. I'd spent an absolutely blameless evening. No – something had evidently gone wrong with the water main during the afternoon. They'd come and mended the pipe, but hadn't had time to make good the paving. They'd just shoved the wood blocks back loose, bashed them down with a – basher – and brushed some sand over the whole thing. Anyway, it produced a perfectly astounding optical illusion. And as if it wasn't realistic enough already, there was a small piece of paper stuck on the road, and it gave a gleam of white just where the collar would be.

Well, as I was walking backwards and forwards across the critical point – that is – the point where the optical illusion ceased to opp, as it were – and you've no idea how startling it was – it's a little difficult to describe.

I don't know whether any of you have ever been to a cinema, but the time I went one of the scenes showed a beautiful maiden sitting on a stone seat by the side of a lake with water lilies and swans and so on, really very fine, and then, before you could say knife, the whole thing sort of dissolved and you found yourself in a low-down eating house in New York, watching a repulsive-looking individual eating spaghetti.

Well that's what it was like and while I was coquet-

ting with this effect – round the corner came a police-
man, very surprised to see me playing, 'Here we go
gathering nuts in May' – er – so early in the morning.
He probably said – 'Here's a gink in a dressing gown.
I'll arrest him – he must be cracked, and I shall get
promoted.'

He came up to me with a certain amount of – hesi-
tation – but I reassured him and said, 'Now you stand
just here and look at that man lying there.' And he
looked and said, 'Well, I'm – something or other,' and
started off up the road – evidently meaning to pick him
up. But in three or four yards he got to the place where
the mirage melted – and then it really was as good as a
play. He looked – and rubbed his eyes – and looked
again. Then he walked to the patch in the road and
examined that. And as soon as he'd decided it wasn't
my fault, I explained to him how dangerous it was,
that all the cars and taxis were shying at it, and one of
them might easily come to grief. *And* they were waking
me up every two minutes. So I said, 'If you'll stop here
and warn things, I'll go across and see Sir William
Horwood in the morning and get him to make you a
sergeant.' And he said, 'I am a sergeant.' So I said,
'Never mind – perhaps he'll make you another.' And I
went back to bed.

At about four o'clock there were noises in the road,
so I got up and looked out and there was my sergeant
and an inspector doing a sort of foxtrot backwards and
forwards – having a great time. No, it wasn't a foxtrot
– it was more of a pavane, which has been described as
a slow and stately dance – the sort of thing they used to
dance in armour. I think they went on playing till it got
light.

Well the next day men came and made a proper job
of the patch in the road – with concrete and tar and so
on – and there it was.

That was in August. Now comes the peculiar part.
Exactly a fortnight ago – at about one in the morning
– there was the same old noise of a car pulling up in a
violent hurry. I was sort of half asleep – and I said,
'There – the same thing's going to go on happening all
night and I shan't get a wink of sleep.' However, this
car didn't drive on as it ought to have done. There were
voices and footsteps and the sound of the car being
backed. General excitement. After a few minutes of
this I got curious – and again went out – in my blue
dressing gown. The car was pulled up just at the same
old place. But there wasn't any optical illusion about it

this time. They'd run over a man and he was very dead. They said he'd walked off the pavement right into them. And now comes the coincidence. He was wearing light brown clothes — not exactly a check pattern, but ruled off into squares, so to speak. You often see girls with cloaks made of that kind of stuff.

# The Rose Garden

## M. R. JAMES

Mr and Mrs Anstruther were at breakfast in the parlour of Westfield Hall, in the county of Essex. They were arranging plans for the day.

'George,' said Mrs Anstruther, 'I think you had better take the car to Maldon and see if you can get any of those knitted things I was speaking about which would do for my stall at the bazaar.'

'Oh well, if you wish it, Mary, of course I can do that, but I had half arranged to play a round with Geoffrey Williamson this morning. The bazaar isn't till Thursday of next week, is it?'

'What has that to do with it, George? I should have thought you would have guessed that if I can't get the things I want in Maldon I shall have to write to all manner of shops in town: and they are certain to send something quite unsuitable in price or quality the first time. If you have actually made an appointment with Mr Williamson, you had better keep it, but I must say I think you might have let me know.'

'Oh no, no, it wasn't really an appointment. I quite see what you mean. I'll go. And what shall you do yourself?'

'Why, when the work of the house is arranged for, I must see about laying out my new rose garden. By the way, before you start for Maldon I wish you would just take Collins to look at the place I fixed upon. You know it, of course.'

'Well, I'm not quite sure that I do, Mary. Is it at the upper end, towards the village?'

'Good gracious no, my dear George; I thought I had

made that quite clear. No, it's that small clearing just off the shrubbery path that goes towards the church.'

'Oh yes, where we were saying there must have been a summer-house once: the place with the old seat and the posts. But do you think there's enough sun there?'

'My dear George, do allow me *some* common sense, and don't credit me with all your ideas about summer-houses. Yes, there will be plenty of sun when we have got rid of some of those box-bushes. I know what you are going to say, and I have as little wish as you to strip the place bare. All I want Collins to do is to clear away the old seats and the posts and things before I come out in an hour's time. And I hope you will manage to get off fairly soon. After luncheon I think I shall go on with my sketch of the church; and if you please you can go over to the links, or –'

'Ah, a good idea – very good! Yes, you finish that sketch, Mary, and I should be glad of a round.'

'I was going to say, you might call on the Bishop; but I suppose it is no use my making *any* suggestion. And now do be getting ready, or half the morning will be gone.'

Mr Anstruther's face, which had shown symptoms of lengthening, shortened itself again, and he hurried from the room, and was soon heard giving orders in the passage. Mrs Anstruther, a stately dame of some fifty summers, proceeded, after a second consideration of the morning's letters, to her housekeeping.

Within a few minutes Mr Anstruther had discovered Collins in the greenhouse, and they were on their way to the site of the projected rose garden. I do not know much about the conditions most suitable to these nurseries, but I am inclined to believe that Mrs Anstruther, though in the habit of describing herself as 'a great gardener', had not been well advised in the selection of a spot for the purpose. It was a small, dank clearing, bounded on one side by a path, and on the other by thick box-bushes, laurels and other evergreens. The ground was almost bare of grass and dark of aspect. Remains of rustic seats and an old and corrugated oak post somewhere near the middle of the clearing had given rise to Mr Anstruther's conjecture that a summer-house had once stood there.

Clearly Collins had not been put in possession of his mistress's intentions with regard to this plot of ground: and when he learnt them from Mr Anstruther he displayed no enthusiasm.

'Of course I could clear them seats away soon enough,' he said. 'They aren't no ornament to the place, Mr Anstruther, and rotten too. Look 'ere, sir' – and he broke off a large piece – 'rotten right through. Yes, clear them away, to be sure we can do that.'

'And the post,' said Mr Anstruther, 'that's got to go too.'

Collins advanced, and shook the post with both hands: then he rubbed his chin.

'That's firm in the ground, that post is,' he said. 'That's been there a number of years, Mr Anstruther. I doubt I shan't get that up not quite so soon as what I can do with them seats.'

'But your mistress specially wishes it to be got out of the way in an hour's time,' said Mr Anstruther.

Collins smiled and shook his head slowly. 'You'll excuse me, sir, but you feel of it for yourself. No, sir, no one can't do what's impossible to 'em, can they, sir? I could git that post up by after tea-time, sir, but that'll want a lot of digging. What you require, you see, sir, if you'll excuse me naming of it, you want the soil loosening round this post 'ere, and me and the boy we shall take a little time doing of that. But now, these 'ere seats,' said Collins, appearing to appropriate this portion of the scheme as due to his own resourcefulness, 'why, I can get the barrer round and 'ave them cleared in, why less than an hour's time from now, if you'll permit of it. Only – '

'Only what, Collins?'

'Well now, it ain't for me to go against orders no more than what it is for you yourself – or anyone else' (this was added somewhat hurriedly), 'but if you'll pardon me, sir, this ain't the place I should have picked out for no rose garden myself. Why, look at them box and laurestinus, 'ow they reg'lar preclude the light from – '

'Ah yes, but we've got to get rid of some of them, of course.'

'Oh, indeed, get rid of them! Yes, to be sure, but – I beg your pardon, Mr Anstruther – '

'I'm sorry, Collins, but I must be getting on now. I hear the car at the door. Your mistress will explain exactly what she wishes. I'll tell her, then, that you can see your way to clearing away the seats at once, and the post this afternoon. Good morning.'

Collins was left rubbing his chin. Mrs Anstruther received the report with some discontent, but did not insist upon any change of plan.

By four o'clock that afternoon she had dismissed her husband to his golf, had dealt faithfully with Collins and with the other duties of the day, and, having sent a campstool and umbrella to the proper spot, had just settled down to her sketch of the church as seen from the shrubbery, when a maid came hurrying down the path to report that Miss Wilkins had called.

Miss Wilkins was one of the few remaining members of the family from whom the Anstruthers had bought the Westfield estate some few years back. She had been staying in the neighbourhood, and this was probably a farewell visit. 'Perhaps you could ask Miss Wilkins to join me here,' said Mrs Anstruther, and soon Miss

Wilkins, a person of mature years, approached.

'Yes, I'm leaving the Ashes tomorrow, and I shall be able to tell my brother how tremendously you have improved the place. Of course he can't help regretting the old house just a little – as I do myself – but the garden is really delightful now.'

'I am so glad you can say so. But you mustn't think we've finished our improvements. Let me show you where I mean to put a rose garden. It's close by here.'

The details of the project were laid before Miss Wilkins at some length; but her thoughts were evidently elsewhere.

'Yes, delightful,' she said at last rather absently. 'But do you know, Mrs Anstruther, I'm afraid I was thinking of old times. I'm *very* glad to have seen just this spot again before you altered it. Frank and I had quite a romance about this place.'

'Yes?' said Mrs Anstruther smilingly; 'do tell me what it was. Something quaint and charming, I'm sure.'

'Not so very charming, but it has always seemed to me curious. Neither of us would ever be here alone when we were children, and I'm not sure that I should care about it now in certain moods. It is one of those things that can hardly be put into words – by me at least – and that sound rather foolish if they are not properly expressed. I can tell you after a fashion what it was that gave us – well, almost a horror of the place when we were alone. It was towards the evening of one very hot autumn day, when Frank had disappeared mysteriously about the grounds, and I was looking for him to fetch him to tea, and going down this path I suddenly saw him, not hiding in the bushes, as I rather expected, but sitting on the bench in the old summer-house – there was a wooden summer-house here, you know – up in the corner, asleep, but with such a dreadful look on his face that I really thought he must be ill or even dead. I rushed at him and shook him, and told him to wake up; and wake up he did, with a scream. I assure you the poor boy seemed almost beside himself with fright. He hurried me away to the house, and was in a terrible state all that night, hardly sleeping. Someone had to sit up with him, as far as I remember. He was better very soon, but for days I couldn't get him to say why he had been in such a condition. It came out at last that he had really been asleep and had had a very odd disjointed sort of dream. He never *saw* much of what was around him, but he *felt* the scenes most vividly. First he made out that he was standing in a large room with a number of people in it, and that someone was opposite to him who was "very powerful", and he was being asked questions which he felt to be very important, and, whenever he answered them, someone – either the person opposite to him, or someone else in the room – seemed to be. as he said, making something up against him. All the voices sounded to him very distant, but he remembered bits of the things that were said: "Where were you on the 19th of October?" and "Is this your handwriting?" and so on. I can see now, of course, that he was dreaming of some trial: but we were never allowed to see the papers, and it was odd that a boy of eight should have such a vivid idea of what went on in a court. All the time he felt, he said, the most intense anxiety and oppression and hopelessness (though I don't suppose he used such words as that to me). Then, after that, there was an interval in which he remembered being dreadfully restless and miserable, and then there came another sort of picture, when he was aware that he had come out of doors on a dark raw morning with a little snow about. It was in a street, or at any rate among houses, and he felt that there were numbers and numbers of people there too, and that he was taken up some creaking wooden steps and stood on a sort of platform, but the only thing he could actually see was a small fire burning somewhere near him. Someone who had been holding his arm left hold of it and went towards this fire, and then he said the fright he was in was worse than at any other part of his dream, and if I had not wakened him up he didn't know what would have become of him. A curious dream for a child to have, wasn't it? Well, so much for that. It must have been later in the year that Frank and I were here, and I was sitting in the arbour just about sunset. I noticed the sun was going down, and told Frank to run in and see if tea was ready while I finished a chapter in the book I was reading. Frank was away longer than I expected, and the light was going so fast that I had to bend over my book to make it out. All at once I became conscious that someone was whispering to me inside the arbour. The only words I could distinguish, or thought I could, were something like "Pull, pull. I'll push, you pull."

'I started up in something of a fright. The voice – it was little more than a whisper – sounded so hoarse and angry, and yet as if it came from a long, long way off – just as it had done in Frank's dream. But, though I was startled, I had enough courage to look round and try to make out where the sound came from. And – this sounds very foolish, I know, but still it is the fact – I made sure that it was strongest when I put my ear to an old post which was part of the end of the seat. I was so certain of this that I remember making some marks on the post – as deep as I could with the scissors out of my work-basket. I don't know why. I wonder, by the way, whether that isn't the very post itself . . . Well, yes, it might be: there *are* marks and scratches on it – but one can't be sure. Anyhow, it was just like that post you have there. My father got to know that both of us had

had a fright in the arbour, and he went down there himself one evening after dinner, and the arbour was pulled down at very short notice. I recollect hearing my father talking about it to an old man who used to do odd jobs in the place, and the old man saying, "Don't you fear for that, sir: he's fast enough in there without no one don't take and let him out." But when I asked who it was, I could get no satisfactory answer. Possibly my father or mother might have told me more about it when I grew up, but, as you know, they both died when we were still quite children. I must say it has always seemed very odd to me, and I've often asked the older people in the village whether they knew of anything strange: but either they knew nothing or they wouldn't tell me. Dear, dear, how I have been boring you with my childish remembrances; but indeed that arbour did absorb our thoughts quite remarkably for a time. You can fancy, can't you, the kind of stories that we made up for ourselves. Well, dear Mrs Anstruther, I must be leaving you now. We shall meet in town this winter, I hope, shan't we?' etc., etc.

The seats and the post were cleared away and uprooted respectively by that evening. Late summer weather is proverbially treacherous, and during dinner-time Mrs Collins sent up to ask for a little brandy, because her husband had taken a nasty chill and she was afraid he would not be able to do much next day.

Mrs Anstruther's morning reflections were not wholly placid. She was sure some roughs had got into the plantation during the night. 'And another thing, George: the moment that Collins is about again, you must tell him to do something about the owls. I never heard anything like them, and I'm positive one came and perched somewhere just outside our window. If it had come in I should have been out of my wits: it must have been a very large bird, from its voice. Didn't you hear it? No, of course not, you were sound asleep as usual. Still, I must say, George, you don't look as if your night had done you much good.'

'My dear, I feel as if another of the same would turn me silly. You have no idea of the dreams I had. I couldn't speak of them when I woke up, and if this room wasn't so bright and sunny I shouldn't care to think of them even now.'

'Well, really, George, that isn't very common with you, I must say. You must have – no, you only had what I had yesterday – unless you had tea at that wretched club house: did you?'

'No, no; nothing but a cup of tea and some bread and butter. I should really like to know how I came to put my dream together – as I suppose one does put one's dreams together from a lot of little things one has been seeing or reading. Look here, Mary, it was like this – if I shan't be boring you –'

'I *wish* to hear what it was, George. I will tell you when I have had enough.'

'All right. I must tell you that it wasn't like other nightmares in one way, because I didn't really *see* anyone who spoke to me or touched me, and yet I was most fearfully impressed with the reality of it all. First I was sitting, no, moving about, in an old-fashioned sort of panelled room. I remember there was a fireplace and a lot of burnt papers in it, and I was in a great state of anxiety about something. There was someone else – a servant, I suppose, because I remember saying to him, "Horses, as quick as you can," and then waiting a bit: and next I heard several people coming upstairs and a noise like spurs on a boarded floor, and then the door opened and whatever it was that I was expecting happened.'

'Yes, but what was that?'

'You see, I couldn't tell: it was the sort of shock that upsets you in a dream. You either wake up or else everything goes black. That was what happened to me. Then I was in a big dark-walled room, panelled, I think, like the other, and a number of people, and I was evidently –'

'Standing your trial, I suppose, George.'

'Goodness! yes, Mary, I was; but did you dream that too? How very odd!'

'No, no; I didn't get enough sleep for that. Go on, George, and I will tell you afterwards.'

'Yes; well, I *was* being tried, for my life, I've no doubt, from the state I was in. I had no one speaking for me, and somewhere there was a most fearful fellow – on the bench, I should have said, only that he seemed to be pitching into me most unfairly, and twisting everything I said, and asking most abominable questions.'

'What about?'

'Why, dates when I was at particular places, and letters I was supposed to have written, and why I had destroyed some papers; and I recollect his laughing at answers I made in a way that quite daunted me. It doesn't sound much, but I can tell you, Mary, it was really appalling at the time. I am quite certain there was such a man once, and a most horrible villain he must have been. The things he said –'

'Thank you, I have no wish to hear them. I can go to the links any day myself. How did it end?'

'Oh, against me; *he* saw to that. I do wish, Mary, I could give you a notion of the strain that came after that, and seemed to me to last for days: waiting and waiting, and sometimes writing things I knew to be enormously important to me, and waiting for answers and none coming, and after that I came out –'

'Ah!'

'What makes you say that? Do you know what sort of thing I saw?'

'Was it a dark cold day, and snow in the streets, and a fire burning somewhere near you?'

'By George, it was! You *have* had the same nightmare! Really not? Well, it is the oddest thing! Yes; I've no doubt it was an execution for high treason. I know I was laid on straw and jolted along most wretchedly, and then had to go up some steps, and someone was holding my arm, and I remember seeing a bit of a ladder and hearing a sound of a lot of people. I really don't think I could bear now to go into a crowd of people and hear the noise they make talking. However, mercifully, I didn't get to the real business. The dream passed off with a sort of thunder inside my head. But, Mary –'

'I know what you are going to ask. I suppose this is an instance of a kind of thought-reading. Miss Wilkins called yesterday and told me of a dream her brother had as a child when they lived here, and something did no doubt make me think of that when I was awake last night listening to those horrible owls and those men talking and laughing in the shrubbery (by the way, I wish you would see if they have done any damage, and speak to the police about it); and so, I suppose, from my brain it must have got into yours while you were asleep. Curious, no doubt, and I am sorry it gave you such a bad night. You had better be as much in the fresh air as you can today.'

'Oh, it's all right now; but I think I *will* go over to the Lodge and see if I can get a game with any of them. And you?'

'I have enough to do for this morning; and this afternoon, if I am not interrupted, there is my drawing.'

'To be sure – I want to see that finished very much.'

No damage was discoverable in the shrubbery. Mr

Anstruther surveyed with faint interest the site of the
rose garden, where the uprooted post still lay, and the
hole it had occupied remained unfilled. Collins, upon
inquiry made, proved to be better, but quite unable to
come to his work. He expressed, by the mouth of his
wife, a hope that he hadn't done nothing wrong clearing away them things. Mrs Collins added that there was
a lot of talking people in Westfield, and the hold ones
was the worst: seemed to think everything of them
having been in the parish longer than what other
people had. But as to what they said no more could
then be ascertained than that it had quite upset Collins,
and was a lot of nonsense.

Recruited by lunch and a brief period of slumber, Mrs
Anstruther settled herself comfortably upon her sketch-
ing chair in the path leading through the shrubbery to
the side-gate of the churchyard. Trees and buildings
were among her favourite subjects, and here she had
good studies of both. She worked hard, and the drawing was becoming a really pleasant thing to look upon
by the time that the wooded hills to the west had shut
off the sun. Still she would have persevered, but the
light changed rapidly, and it became obvious that the
last touches must be added on the morrow. She rose
and turned towards the house, pausing for a time to
take delight in the limpid green western sky. Then she
passed on between the dark box-bushes, and, at a point
just before the path debouched on the lawn, she stopped
once again and considered the quiet evening landscape,
and made a mental note that that must be the tower of
one of the Roothing churches that one caught on the
sky-line. Then a bird (perhaps) rustled in the box-bush
on her left, and she turned and started at seeing what
at first she took to be a Fifth of November mask peep-

ing out among the branches. She looked closer.

It was not a mask. It was a face -- large, smooth, and pink. She remembers the minute drops of perspiration which were starting from its forehead : she remembers how the jaws were clean-shaven and the eyes shut. She remembers also, and with an accuracy which makes the thought intolerable to her, how the mouth was open and a single tooth appeared below the upper lip. As she looked the face receded into the darkness of the bush. The shelter of the house was gained and the door shut before she collapsed.

Mr and Mrs Anstruther had been for a week or more recruiting at Brighton before they received a circular from the Essex Archæological Society, and a query as to whether they possessed certain historical portraits which it was desired to include in the forthcoming work on Essex Portraits, to be published under the Society's auspices. There was an accompanying letter from the Secretary which contained the following passage : 'We are specially anxious to know whether you possess the original of the engraving of which I enclose a photograph. It represents Sir —— ——, Lord Chief Justice under Charles II, who, as you doubtless know, retired after his disgrace to Westfield, and is supposed to have died there of remorse. It may interest you to hear that a curious entry has recently been found in the registers, not of Westfield but of Priors Roothing, to the effect that the parish was so much troubled after his death that the rector of Westfield summoned the parsons of all the Roothings to come and lay him; which they did. The entry ends by saying : "The stake is in a field adjoining to the churchyard of Westfield, on the west side." Perhaps you can let us know if any tradition to this effect is current in your parish.'

The incidents which the 'enclosed photograph' recalled were productive of a severe shock to Mrs Anstruther. It was decided that she must spend the winter abroad.

Mr Anstruther, when he went down to Westfield to make the necessary arrangements, not unnaturally told his story to the rector (an old gentleman), who showed little surprise.

'Really I had managed to piece out for myself very much what must have happened, partly from old people's talk and partly from what I saw in your grounds. Of course we have suffered to some extent also. Yes, it was bad at first: like owls, as you say, and men talking sometimes. One night it was in this garden, and at other times about several of the cottages. But lately there has been very little: I think it will die out. There is nothing in our registers except the entry of the burial, and what I for a long time took to be the family motto; but last time I looked at it I noticed that it was added in a later hand and had the initials of one of our rectors quite late in the seventeenth century, A. C. – Augustine Crompton. Here it is, you see – *quieta non movere*.* I suppose – Well, it is rather hard to say exactly what I do suppose.'

\* Free translation: 'Let sleeping dogs lie.'

# Ghost Riders of the Sioux

KENNETH ULYATT

I suppose I saw the ghost riders afore anyone else in the valley.

It was the time between supper and bed. Ma had told me to sit and read. She was always on about schooling but I'd no sooner picked up my reading book and settled against the back wall of the house to get the last of the sun afore it went behind the hills when Dave come by. He had a gun and his dog, Jim, and it was that dog and ours that started us off up the valley. They don't agree; never did and they was fighting and snarling and kicking up an awful ruckus so that soon Ma hollered out of the kitchen to get them tarnation animals parted and clear off so folks could have peace after eating.

Reckon she forgot about schooling!

Dave and I didn't want no pushing. I tied our Sam up in the barn and we lit out up the valley, his dog, Jim, bouncing ahead and snuffing at the scrub and pretending he'd smelled a cottontail while I asked Dave if I could carry the gun. Of course, he wouldn't let me.

'It's loaded.'

'I won't touch the trigger, honest.'

'There ain't no safety catch. It's busted.'

'I'll be careful, Dave. Pa's taught me how to handle our new gun.'

'What new gun? I never knowed you got a new gun.'

'It's a Winchester. It can fire . . . twenty shots a minute.' I was guessing, of course, to put on a show. Dave was two years older'n me. He knew most things, like where the railroad ran after Potter's Point and how far it was to Oregon and how many steers there was in the whole of our valley . . . and he had this gun.

'Let me carry it, Dave.'

'When we get up the valley.'

I shut up then. I knew that meant not never. When we got up the valley, he'd say: 'We ain't far enough up yet,' and so it would go on until we turned back and then there'd be some other reason so that I wouldn't get to carry the gun at all. I didn't care. It was a rotten old gun, anyway.

But to get back to the ghost riders.

We scouted along the stream, Dave making a great play of seeing beaver and levelling the gun. But he never fired it and I began to reckon that there weren't no bullets in it, anyway.

The sun had gone down by this time and it was sort of half light, with deep shadows beneath the trees so that you didn't rightly want to go too far into the scrub. We'd just decided to turn back when Jim started to growl.

Now that dog had been growling and snuffling ever since we left the house. If there was a stone in the path or a tuft of hair hanging on a bush where some steer had passed he'd raise a barking like it was a cottontail pulling a long nose at him. But he'd been quiet by the stream and when we reached the glade about two miles from the house he'd got to padding along at our heels while Dave decided that it wasn't the right night for a hunt after all and we turned back to look down the valley.

Ma had put a lamp in the window and it glowed yellow all that way off. From across the valley you could hear the bellow of some stray calf looking for its mother.

'C'mon, Jim.'

Dave looked back at the dog. 'What's got into him?'

I turned to look, too. The creature was at the top of a steep slope that made the lip of the glade we was standing in. He leaned forward, his tail stiff behind him and his muzzle pointing direct at the dark trees beyond.

'Here, boy.' Dave put on a gruff, commanding voice but the dog didn't move.

The shadows seemed to creep closer while we waited.

Then Jim gave a sort of whine. His tail dropped lower until it crept, trembling, between his back legs. The hair all along his back was bristling up and his whole body was shaking.

'It's a bear. Pa said there was bears in the hills.'

'Ain't no bear,' said Dave. 'If it was a bear we'd have smelled it.' But he was worried just the same and he levelled the old gun and made to move up the slope.

We inched forward as the dog went down on its belly. A coldness had come into the air as if it was night already.

At the top of the slope there was nothing, just the shadows of the trees up there and the white trunks of the birches shining. And then one of them moved!

Dave jumped back so quick he cannoned into me and we both fell on the grass. The dog, disturbed by the clatter, sprang to its feet and leaped forward with a barking you could've heard a mile off. From where we was sprawling on the ground you couldn't see him, but you could hear him plenty.

Then suddenly that barking changed to a shriek of pain. I'd seen a dog get caught once in a harrow that some dirt farmer had on the other side of the valley and it sounded like that. He came over the top of the slope still yowling but it was one long moaning cry now and he blundered into us as we scrambled for the gun.

He was wet, but whether from slavering so much or

what I didn't know then. All I knew was Dave shaking my arm and pointing up the glade. He didn't speak.

They stood there, white against the blackness that was coming down fast. They swayed together and moaned and the trees seemed to go from side to side with them.

We got to hell outa there, as one of the hired hands said. Although Ma reckoned I shouldn't use such words that's just what we did. Later, the old gun roared out. Dave said he fired when he first saw them but I reckon he tripped when we run and it went off. It didn't have no safety catch anyhow.

We got clear of the trees and pounded down the path to that welcoming light. A mile farther on I stumbled over something and fell.

It was Jim. He was lying stretched on the dirt, his head pointed to the house and his legs drawn back under him like he was still trying to run when he dropped. There was blood all over his side and he was dead.

We carried him back to the house and we was pretty bloody by the time Ma opened the door, exclaiming about where we had been and what sense was there in firing off a gun at that time of night. Then she saw the blood and Dave was crying now because Jim was dead and I guess I cried too, 'cause we was safe back home and they hadn't caught us.

'Who didn't catch you?' Pa was impatient. He stooped down and peered into my face and asked again but I couldn't say any more and the tears came up inside.

'Leave the boy alone, Mark,' said Ma. 'Can't you see he's frightened out of his wits, and the dog dead, too.'

She dragged us near the fire and sat us down. There was a smell of meat coming from the pot on the range and pretty soon we was both more hungry than scared.

When Mr Hannery, Dave's Pa, come in we was drinking the last of our bowls of soup and only the dead dog by the back door told him that something was amiss.

'I shot at him, Pa, but he kept comin'.' Dave still pushed the story about shooting at what we had seen up the valley and I didn't let on that I thought the gun had gone off by accident. When it come for me to tell my part I just let them think we had stopped to fire back at what was chasing us.

'But who was after you?' Pa asked again, waving Ma back now that she had had her say and we was sitting there all warm with a good soup inside us even if it was tomorrow's dinner.

'They was all white, Pa. Come out of the trees an' killed th' dog an' would've killed us too if we hadn't run.' Dave told most of the story again and they listened to him more; after all, he was older'n me and he worked for his Pa on their ranch like any other man – or so he said.

To me, thinking back, it was just something white that had moved among the birch trunks. I wasn't sure that anybody'd really come after us 'though I'd been plenty scared and hadn't stopped long enough to look, after that first glimpse.

But the dog was killed, wasn't he. Deader'n a stick, I heard someone say.

'It's a knife.' Mr Hannery's voice drifted through the door. 'Now, who'd 've killed a dog like that?'

'Perhaps we'd better go and look, Tom,' I heard my Pa answer and presently they rode off, taking our hound with them and two of the hands from the bunkhouse.

But they never found nothing beyond a few hoofprints across the top of the valley. Unshod, they was. Could've been wild ponies – even Indians, though it was ten year since the Sioux come this far south. Mr Hannery picked up a small pellet of red stuff – 'ochre', he said it was but it looked like dirt to me and nobody thought much of it. They was all too busy looking for some drifter who could've killed the dog.

But I know now that they was ghost riders. And the white shirts they was wearing was the first sign of the troubles that was to come.

That was the summer the chinook come on real hot.

There was always a warm wind up the valley, on and off through the summer months, but this was different. It just kept on coming; off the badlands, south of the Black Hills, Pa said. The little garden Ma growed behind the house just curled up and died and the farmers in the valley lost their oats and wheat and vegetables.

Even the range grass burned up in the heat.

Dave said that in Nebraska the homesteaders were packing up and going back east; leaving the farms they'd come west to get 'cause nothing would grow there that year.

It was bad for us, too. Pa lost a lot of stock. They just dropped dead out on the range when the water ran out. I used to lie on the bed on top of the covers and listen to the shutters banging and the old house creaking in the wind. And all the time the old windmill that Pa had made squeaked and groaned and turned and sucked up water from deep down. Hundreds of feet deep that well was. An old Indian well. And it was this old well that saved us, I guess.

The river stopped running and was just a mess of pot-hole ponds with stag-edy water and scum on the top that even the cattle wouldn't touch – at first. And skeeters in clouds, 'though they died off, too, as the summer and the hot wind went on and on.

I think it was because things was so bad that Dave and I got to make the trip north with Takawa. We

would never have gone on our own if everyone hadn't
been so busy fighting the drought. We went to see some
folks of Dave's just south of the Cheyenne fork, about
two days' ride from our own White River.

'You ain't letting them go off alone and the hills all
burnt up like this?' Ma asked, in a sort of high voice
that was not at all like her usual tone.

Dave had come over with the ponies and a message
from Mr Hannery and he stood in the sun, trailing the
reins and looking from her to Pa who was standing by
him. Ma had a ladle in one hand, the other was on her
hip. And when she stood like that she usually got her
own way. I was thinking that I wouldn't get to go on
the trip when Pa spoke out, sharp like. 'Boy's got to
learn to stand on his own feet, Sarah. He'll be all right.
They know the road an' they'll stop over at the Colbys'
for th' night. It's all been arranged.'

'Yeah. Pa says he's sending 'Kawa with us so we can
bring back the ponies Uncle Jack's givin' us. An' *he*
won't get lost.' Dave put his bit in, like it was carefully
thought out and I guess it was, really. Mr Hannery and
Pa wouldn't have let us go off if there'd been any like-
lihood of trouble.

Though, of course, they didn't know about the ghost
riders then.

Maybe it was the hot day, maybe it was because
things had begun to get on top of her, but Ma gave in.
First time I knowed her to do it.

'All right. You know what I think. But all right. Go
ahead.' And she waved the ladle in the air and went
back into the kitchen.

'Yippee!'

I let out a scream and lit off for the barn where old
Sam was lying in the shade and just for devilment I
rolled him over and scattered straw over him so that he
sneezed with the dust like I knowed he would.

Dave helped me saddle the pony and waited while I begged Ma pack me a bed roll and something to eat. We left, waving back all the while until the house was small and shimmering in the distance and only the windmill stuck up sharp in the haze.

Takawa was already at the Hannerys' when we got there. He was about the only Indian I'd ever knowed except his folks, of course, who lived on the far side of the valley where the ground was poor and they scratched a living.

Takawa's father was a breed who worked for Dave's Pa. His wife was a full-blood Sioux and there was a tribe of kids, younger'n me, except for Takawa, who was about the same age as Dave.

Takawa never came near the house except sometimes when Pa told the breed he could take this or that from the ranch; usually something we had finished with or didn't want. Then Takawa and his old man would come with their mule and hitch the stores or whatever it was up on the old aparejo pack and that's the last we'd see of them round the house.

He was a straight, willowy boy, dark brown. But then so were we with the sun. Except when we took our clothes off and went swimming you could see he wasn't the same, he was dark all over.

We left about noon, going north up the valley. Soon you could see the tops of the Black Hills away to our left as the ground flattened out and began to give way to the plains proper.

I'd never been out on the range before on my own. I'd been to Cheyenne and Pierre and, once even, to Custer City, but that was with Pa. It was a funny feeling, being all alone in all that space; just rolling grass as far as you could see, bending and swaying in the hot wind.

Takawa rode ahead and didn't speak much. Dave and

I followed, riding side by side and making out we was pioneers crossing the country for the first time and that there was Indians watching us. Pretty soon I got to half believing that there really was Indians out on the plains with us but Dave said that the agents kept them north on the reservations and that they daren't come out now 'cause of the soldiers.

The ride was tame, really. The trail was marked with stones and afore long we could see the country dripping down to the big river and the tops of the trees by the Colby place where we was to spend the night.

Dave's uncle lived at Plum Creek, just where the Cheyenne turned east. Towards the Missouri, Dave said, waving an arm at the cottonwoods and aspens that trailed along the river.

'Over there's Standing Rock,' says Dave's Uncle Jack, who'd just come up at that moment. 'Pierre first, then, where there's a sort of blue haze, that's Standing Rock Reservation where old Sitting Bull's been kept since he come back from Canada.'

'When did he go to Canada, and why?' asked Dave.

'Just after you was born, lad,' answered Uncle Jack. 'The Sioux had killed Custer and half his regiment and the soldiers chased them right up to the border. Old Sitting Bull stayed in Canada best part of four year afore he reckoned it was safe to come back. Now they keep him pinned down on the reservation at Standing Rock.'

He waved a hand over our heads, making a big curve.

'Ten year ago this was all Sioux country. Then th' Gov'nment bought th' Black Hills and opened it up for settlement. We're right in the middle of the reservations here. Standing Rock to the north; Brulé to the east and Pine Ridge, south there, behind your home range, Davy.'

Takawa was standing a little way off, looking to the

blue hills in the north.

'Do th' Injuns ever come here, Uncle Jack?'

'They ain't allowed to travel off th' reservation without permission, though they do. Party came by here early this summer. Bin all th' way down to Nevada, I hear. Injuns ride th' railroads, too; whole parties go off on a trip to see relatives, just like you come up to see us.'

The evening light was beginning to come down by this time and as we went back to the ranch I was reminded of the time we'd seen the ghost riders up the valley.

We were going back the next day, so we went to bed early. All the same it was a good evening, with a big supper Dave's Aunt Betty had specially got for us and a fiddler and folks riding over to visit. After we got to bed we lay there for some time with the music still ringing in our heads.

'You seen many Injuns, Dave?'

'Course I have. Went over to Pine Ridge once with Pa and 'Kawa's old man, didn't we, 'Kawa?'

The Indian boy had a bed at the end of the room. Dave's aunt had given him a hard look when we come but then, I suppose seeing we'd come to no harm so far, made him up a bed in the room with us. He lay with his hands behind his head, looking through the window at the stars and he grunted in answer to Dave's question.

We talked for a while and then, one by one, we went to sleep. In the morning we said our 'goodbyes' and set off, driving the ponies before us. We played at being on a cattle drive for most of the morning until we got tired of it. Then we just pushed silently on and it got hotter and hotter.

We passed several pot-hole ponds, all dried up and the ducks and marsh birds gone and the mud cracked so you could ride across the bottom like it was a road. The river was away to our right and when we stopped to eat the pie that Dave's aunt had given us we watched the ponies snuffing at the burnt grass and pointing their heads at the trees in the distance as though they could smell water.

'I reckon we won't make Colbys' tonight,' said Dave, suddenly. 'Look at 'em. We'd better camp by the river where they can get freshed up. What do you say, 'Kawa?'

'Your father said we were not to camp – that we should stay at Captain Colby's both nights,' said the Indian boy, gravely.

'Yeah, I know, but we'll be all right.' Dave looked at me. 'No good bringing in half-dead ponies. Why they might jest drop afore we could get 'em home if we don't stop for water.'

It was late afternoon and certainly hot. The sun beat in our faces and when the chinook let up, as it did from time to time, flies buzzed black on the remains of the pie. Far off, across the trees, there was a dust cloud where someone was probably moving cattle down to the river for the night.

It seemed the right thing to do 'though I knowed what Pa would have said. Still, Pa wasn't there, so we headed for the river and after we'd watered the ponies we moved back to some high ground where the trees reached out on to the edge of the plain. It was a funny grey light now that the sun had gone and I was mighty glad when Takawa lit a fire and we huddled round it on our blankets.

The wind, instead of dying like it usually does in the evening, just kept on, rocking the branches above our heads.

Out there on the plains with no one around for hundreds of miles – or so Dave said, though I hadn't reckoned we'd come more than forty mile from home myself

— it took a long time to get to sleep. And when I did it seemed only a minute afore I was awake again. Not drowsy-awake, like you are the first time you open your eyes in the morning. But wide awake and sitting up and clutching my blanket round my middle.

And scared.

I could see the others were awake too. Though it seemed we'd only just bedded down it must have been near dawn. It was dark; that thick darkness that comes just afore the sun comes up.

And right away I knew that it was the same darkness that had surrounded us in the glade when the ghost riders had killed Dave's dog.

The tree trunks stood out dimly against the blackness and the branches rustled slightly above our heads. But the wind had dropped and in its place was what had awakened us all.

It was a sort of moaning noise that went up and down and didn't stop and it made the hair on the back of my neck stand up and my skin sort of creep. The ponies were restless and pulling at their tethers.

And the ground, when I leaned on it with my elbow, trembled.

'What is it?'

Dave's voice was hoarse and he had to swallow afore he could speak.

'I dunno. I just waked up.'

He was fumbling for the gun under the blankets.

''Kawa! 'Kawa! You awake?'

The Indian boy looked at us from across the dead fire. I could see the whites of his eyes, rolling. He didn't answer or stir from his blankets.

'C'mon!'

Dave shuffled up, dragging on his jacket and tugging at his belt. He rested the gun against his knee and I knew, as he looked round, that the ghosts of the valley was in his mind, too.

We scrambled to our feet and stood undecided. We could see nothing, but the awful moaning noise went on and on, rising higher now and then lulling off.

'C'mon, 'Kawa. Git up.'

Dave pulled the blankets from the Indian boy and, kneeling down, shook him violently, all the while looking over his shoulder this way and that as if he half expected the ghost riders to come sweeping down on the camp.

Takawa was plenty scared, too. I could see that he just wanted to bury his head under the blankets and shut that moaning out of his ears. I guess I wanted to, as well, but Dave wouldn't have any. I'll give him credit. There was danger, we all knew, and Dave wanted us to be ready to meet it. I reckon Mr Hannery would've been proud of him.

But our thoughts was a long way from home, that cosy, safe place that we'd kicked against so often. The ghost riders was mighty near and, suddenly, a long shriek tore through the blackness and brought Takawa to his feet with a great jump. He stood shaking so much that I could feel it, though I weren't within arm's length of him.

'Take this, and come on.'

Dave had whirled round at the shrieking to face the gloomy trees. The fire was out. The sky was dark. Nothing moved, but beyond the slope, beyond the fringe of cottonwoods the whole night seemed to be shuddering.

Takawa clutched at the knife that Dave was holding out and then we went scrambling up the slope beyond the ponies. I had the rifle Pa had given me for the trip – the old breech-loader that he'd let me use since we got the Winchester and I hugged it close. It was a comfort, 'though I forgot it weren't loaded and that the cartridges was down there in the saddlebag by the fire!

At the top of the slope Dave sprawled down and crawled under some bushes. Out away from the open space round the fire, it didn't seem so bad.

'What is it? What're we goin' to do?'

'I dunno. It's them ghost riders again, I know it is.'

Dave jerked in the dark as another shriek rang out. It seemed to come from over the rise. We huddled down closer. Below, the ponies bunched and turned and pulled at the ropes.

While we lay there, undecided, there come a glimmer of light from beyond the ridge, as if someone had stirred a fire to flame, then doused it again. The moaning stopped. Then a voice wailed and all the moaning swept up in answer. And a drumming started and the trembling feeling in the earth seemed to be coming right up underneath us.

All this time Dave had been making up his mind. He'd been plenty scared that night back in the valley when we'd run and ashamed, afterwards, I guess. Now he was going to make up for it and 'though I was scared and Takawa weren't much help I was with him.

'There ain't no such thing as ghosts.' Dave was saying what my Pa and Mr Hannery had told us, his voice tight and sort of high. 'I'm goin' t'see.'

Left to me, I would have high-tailed it out of the place but Dave gave me no time to argue and rather than be left alone with a frightened Indian boy I scrambled up the slope after him, dragging my empty gun.

Of course, Takawa followed. I knew he was following for I could feel his breath on my legs when we stopped crawling to get over a tree stump and I could see his wide eyes when I looked back, very close to me. Pretty soon, I bumped into Dave's feet. We were near the top of the ridge and it had got lighter and I crawled round Dave and lay down beside him. Dave's hand gripped my shoulder so hard I nearly cried out. Then I looked down the dark slope where the ground was clear and the earth moved.

And I froze stiff.

I can't never forget that moment. Even now, when it's all over and I know what it was, I still wake up sweating some nights and see the drifting smoke and the ghosts swarming up out of the hole beyond the buffalo skull. The light had begun to creep over the hills and the first thing I saw was a tall leaning pole and hanging at the top, a bunch of arms that moved slowly in time to the drumming and shaking.

There was a white mist that spread all before us, curling and twisting out of some great heap on the ground. A heap which moved and cried and hissed. And below the pole was a great gathering of ghosts, all white and shining like we had seen in the valley. And they seemed to be sinking down and then rising up and all the time crying out in the most horrible tones I ever heard.

I couldn't move after I saw them; I just lay there holding my gun and trembling. My mouth was dry and I tried to shut my eyes to keep out the sight but I couldn't. Takawa's body was shaking against mine and even Dave's mouth hung open and his fingers was letting the rifle slip.

So there *was* ghosts and Pa and Mr Hannery was *wrong*!

How long we lay there I don't know, but it got lighter and the smoke or mist kept billowing up out of the hole and every so often another ghost would come out and join the rest and dance horribly.

As the noise got wilder we sank lower and lower into the bushes. Then a great shout went up, followed by a quiet so still I could hear my heart beating and the others', too. We scrambled back a bit, Dave shuffling alongside me, and it was only afterwards that I realized we'd left Takawa on the ridge, alone.

The shrieking burst out afresh and a terrible thing happened. The ghosts began to run in all directions, crying out and falling and rolling and heaving on the ground. And we could see plainer now, 'though we didn't want to, and other ghosts with horrible, swirling faces and white bodies moving with the signs of birds and animals all mixed up and butting the trees and laying stiff or kicking on the ground with other ghosts bending over them doing heaven knows what.

Quite sudden, as I knew it must afore long, one loomed out of the mist above us. Maybe it was 'cause I was lying on the ground but it was taller than ever I saw, with white and red on its face and eyes that seemed to bulge. It stood over Takawa and its arm was raised as though it was going to beat him into the ground. It couldn't see us, for we had rolled into the bushes. And it screamed at Takawa and the Indian boy got slowly up and faced it.

He had guts, Dave said, afterwards. Me, I would have laid there and covered my ears and eyes but Takawa, who was the most frightened of us all, rose up to face whatever it was that had come out of the mist to find us.

For a moment they stood against the reddening sky. Then the ghost screeched again and was gone and Takawa, half-running, half-sliding, came down the slope and made for the camp. We followed and when we got there the Indian boy was grabbing the blankets and packing the gear.

The moaning had stopped and it was light and because we could see  the ponies and the packs and was getting ready to go, it all felt better.

We went out on to the plain, anywhere, away from
the cottonwoods, leading the ponies, flying along, not
caring much whether we lost them or not. We left the
cooking pot and the plates but we didn't think of this
till we was a long ways out and the sun was up.

It was a breathless ride. I didn't know where we was
or where we was heading. All I knowed was that we'd
got away from the ghost dancers. But Takawa led the
way. Somehow he was different. Not frightened any
more  Yet he'd been closer than anyone.

When we got near to the Colbys' we reined in and talked about what we'd tell them. Dave was for keeping it quiet and Takawa just sat silent, not looking at us and not joining in the talk. But I knew that we should have been back at the Colbys' place for the night and that there'd be questions. And I guess I knew that the sight of the ghost riders would still be on our faces.

So we told them. Everything we could remember and Captain Colby looked at us for a long time after we'd finished but said nothing. I didn't know whether he believed us or not.

Then he collected some of the hands and sent a messenger towards Custer City and rode back the way we had come himself, while Mrs Colby cooked us breakfast and Takawa sat outside in the shade of the house and wouldn't talk. He wouldn't even talk to Captain Colby when the Captain asked him to describe the ghost he'd seen close up. Not anything.

Well, they didn't find much. They brought back a long pole with tattered strips of rag hanging from it. They'd found a buffalo skull looking into the hole in the mound where the smoke had come from. And some pellets of red ochre near the ashes of a fire. I heard them say there was a big circle where the ground had been flattened by stamping but I didn't think ghosts weighed heavy and said so.

Captain Colby smiled and said what my Pa had said, that there weren't such things as ghosts.

But he sent two riders back with us and they come right into the valley and talked long with Pa. Ma made a fuss of me and went on at Pa for letting us go. But we was back home and safe, 'though I still didn't know what it was all about.

'Shirts that stop bullets? There ain't no such thing.'

'That's what he says.'

Dave stubbed his stick into the ground. I knowed he didn't like it when I went against him, but this story was nonsense. I didn't say any more and presently he began to trace the outline of a man in the dust. Then he dug the point of his stick into it just where the heart would have been and said: 'The shirts have got some sort of power woven into 'em. They turn the bullets aside. That's what Takawa says.'

'Has he got one of these shirts?' I asked Dave.

It was almost two weeks since we got back from the trip to Dave's uncle. Takawa had gone off that same night and we hadn't seen him again till Dave come over this afternoon I'm telling about now.

'He says they weren't ghosts we saw, they was Injuns and that they had these magic shirts on that made 'em look like ghosts. I knew they weren't ghosts,' he added, scuffling the stick in the dirt.

That wasn't what he had told Captain Colby, but I didn't say so. We went off up the creek and found Takawa sitting by one of the pools and staring down into the water. He was throwing a stick into it from time to time and at first he wouldn't talk but after a while he looked at us and began a sort of speech.

All the time he was talking he was different. I don't know what it was about him but he had a calm, strong – yes, that was it, a *strong* look. Before, he'd always been just an Indian boy who nobody in the valley thought much about and who lived there just because we let him. Now he had changed and he told us a strange story about what was going to happen and who the ghost riders really were.

Long ago, all the land had belonged to the Indians, began Takawa. There had been no white people at all and the tribes had hunted and followed the buffalo; so many buffalo that they spread like black clouds over the prairie. And this old life was a good life with no sickness or disease and everyone was happy.

Takawa paused and looked into the pool for so long that I thought he wasn't going to tell us no more. Then he went on: the Whites came from the east and killed off the buffalo and took the land. They put the Indians into shacks on reservations, which was just land that nothing would grow on and was no good to them, anyway.

A new land was coming for the Indian, he said. It was already on its way from the west and would reach our valley about next year. And when it came there would be a signal. The ground would tremble.

Dave and I looked at each other, startled.

At this signal, Takawa went on, the Indians would fix sacred eagle's feathers into their hair and rise up above while the new land rolled east and pushed the Whites back into the sea from where they'd come. After this, the Indians would let themselves down on the new land and there they would find all the Indians who had ever lived before. Friends and relations long dead and who were now alive again. And they would all be happy leading the old life.

'All the nations of the Indian coming home,' Takawa almost sang it and swayed from side to side as he did so. On every hand there would be herds of deer and antelope and the buffalo would once more blacken the prairie.

'And the ghost riders and the shirts,' cried Dave. 'Go on, tell about them.'

The Indian boy looked straight at me and although it was near noon I shivered.

'The ghost riders come from Wovoka, who is a great shaman and who will lead us to the new land. He is the son of God who the white men killed and nailed to a cross.'

'Jesus?' I said. 'You mean Jesus, in the Bible?'

'He has the marks on his hands and feet,' replied Takawa, 'and he can work great magic. He has caused rain to fall in the dry season and ice to appear in the river in summer.

'And he has given the Sioux ghost shirts that will turn away the soldiers' bullets.'

'How do you know all this, 'Kawa?'

'Many chiefs went from the reservation to see. He gave them the magic paint for the signs on the shirts and he taught them the ghost dance by which the Indian can see this new land before it comes and help to bring it about.'

Well, that was Takawa's story. And Dave and I talked it over and I reckoned we'd better ask Pa. I didn't think he'd believe us or even want to listen but he took it mighty serious and spoke like I'd never heard him speak before to me. Straight out, as if I was a man.

'You must speak up, Ben, tell everything you know. Not just to me but to Captain Colby and everyone else.'

'Captain Colby ain't here.'

'No, but he will be tonight, and so will many others.'

That night, when Dave and I got back from some chore round the meadows, Ma called us in. There was more horses tied up outside the house than I'd seen for a long whiles and the big room was full of men. Some of them I knowed, like Mr Hannery and Captain Colby. But there were others I didn't, and more than one blue uniform.

We had to tell everything, standing there by the table. About the ghost riders we'd seen up the valley in the spring and about the ghost dancers that we'd stumbled on on that summer trip to Dave's Uncle Jack. Every little detail, right down to the paintings on the ghosts and the sort of noise they made.

After we'd finished there was a long silence.

'That first bunch must have been Big Foot and his party, comin' back from Nevada,' said a voice from the corner where I couldn't see.

'When they first brought stories of this Wovoka to th' reservations,' added someone else.

Captain Colby nodded. 'They went down two months before with the agent's permission. It was when they returned that it all started.'

' 'Kawa told us about Wovoka,' I blurted out. 'Said he was like Jesus.'

I looked round, a bit scared, but no one, not even Pa, told me to hold my tongue.

'Wovoka is a Paiute sheep-herder down in Nevada, Ben,' said Captain Colby quietly. 'He has dreams of a new world coming for the Indians and he teaches them a dance to make these dreams come true.'

'But the ghosts? We saw the ghosts in the smoke.'

An old man leaned forward and spoke gently.

'They weren't ghosts, Ben, they was Injuns. And it was steam, not smoke. They heat stones and put them in a big hut covered tight with leaves and then they throw water over the stones and sit in the steam to purify themselves. It's an old custom. Then they put on the white shirts and paint themselves with red ochre.'

'And then they dance and sing this song about the coming of the Indian nations,' said another voice. 'They dance till they go into a trance and see a vision of the new land that they think is coming.'

There was more general talking now but I wasn't listening. I was thinking of the ghost dancers and the way they had rolled on the ground and butted the trees. And the terrible shrieking.

'. . . what I cannot understand,' it was Captain Colby speaking and he brought my mind back to the crowded room, '. . . what I cannot understand is the thought *behind* this teaching. It goes against all the Indians hold dear. They've always rated success in war as a man's highest achievement. This sheep-herder's preaching peace. All the Indians have to do is to follow the ten commandments and the old life will return a hundred times better.'

He paused and cleared his throat. Somebody put in from the back of the room in a big booming voice: 'Then it's a better religion he's offering the tribes than all our teachings have accomplished in a hundred years.'

That was Mr Farley who preached on the Sabbath and if he was getting into it there was going to be more long words and stuff I wouldn't understand. But there was one more thing I did hear before Ma took me out.

It was Captain Colby speaking and his voice was hard.

'If the Sioux have got hold of it it won't mean peace. It'll be twisted to mean war, and war on the Whites. It's been a hard, dry summer. Food's scarce on the reservations and the hunting's poor. The Sioux have been down a long time – they're ready to clutch at anything.'

And as I went out of the door, with Ma sweeping through all those men and them, for once, not even noticing her and standing aside like they usually do, I heard another voice shouting:

'Then we want soldiers in all the towns round the reservations – and an end to these ghost dances!'

We sat in the kitchen till the meeting broke up and Mr Hannery come in for Dave. I stood on the porch and watched the horses move off up the road, all white in the moonlight.

Like ghosts themselves, they were.

Next thing that happened was the soldiers coming through the valley. It must have been two-three month after the meeting 'cause the drought had broken and I remembered the creek was running so they came splashing over the ford and turned south, down the trail.

I'd ridden like fury to fetch Dave, soon as I knew they was coming. I liked to be the first to tell, sometimes, and he was sure keen to see them. We sat on our ponies on the ridge and watched. And we waved and some of the soldiers waved back.

It was a good sight: the sun flashed on the bridles and the harness jingled. There must have been three hundred or more, I reckon.

'Look,' cried Dave. 'Lookit that gun on wheels.'

It rolled behind the column, just before the wagon train, pulled by a black team and flashing its brass bands and long thin barrel.

We sat there till they was out of sight and then turned towards home.

'Goin' to Pine Ridge, I shouldn't wonder,' said Dave.

There was an Army horse at the house when I got back and Ma was in a tizzy, shouting at me to ride off and get Pa who was over the other side of the hill, branding the new steers which had been shared out in the big valley round-up. When we got back Ma was making a big show like she does when a stranger comes. There was china on the table and the big, old tea-pot with flowers on it that she'd brought from her home when she was first married. We didn't see that often.

The man rose to greet Pa and they shook hands. He was an officer, I guess, with gold braid on his shoulders and a trimming to his hat which was lying on the table.

'It's been a long time,' said Pa.

'Four years,' answered the officer, smiling. 'Your boy's grown.'

Ma beamed and Pa nodded, rubbing my hair like he does sometimes. I stepped away and then Ma said: 'Get along, Ben. Men want to talk.'

That was always the way when strangers come. They'd want to talk and I'd want to listen. And usually I got sent away. When I grow up and get me a son I'll never send him away when strangers come.

I hung around the house but couldn't hear anything and I was swinging on the gate when the soldier stepped out and mounted up. He had a hand-gun strapped to his belt and it thumped as he swung into the saddle. He had a rifle in the scabbard on his horse but then so did most riders in the valley, these days. It was the hand-gun and holster that I'd not seen close up.

He looked at me hanging on the gate.

'Ever seen real wild Indians, Ben?' he asked.

'No.'

'No, *sir*,' said Ma.

'No, sir.'

'Know what year it is, Ben?'

'1889, sir.'

'What year were you born?'

I didn't answer.

'Well, how old are you now?'

'Eleven, sir.'

The officer looked at Pa and then back at me. 'Custer was long dead an' the war finished before you came here. No wonder the boy knows nothing of Indians.' He raised a hand. 'Well, good-bye, Ben.' I saluted back. He took off his hat to Ma. 'Remember, Ma'am. Keep close to the house.' He pointed at me. 'Him, too.'

'We'll see he stays in the valley,' said Pa.

'Within sound of the iron,' added Ma, grimly, striking the triangle that hung from a beam of the porch roof and was used to call the hands to eat. Old Sam came out of the barn, wagging his tail.

The officer waved and rode off, not the way he had come but north, for the Hannery place.

I followed Ma into the house. 'What is it, Ma? Why can't I go out of the valley?'

'Because there may be trouble, that's why. Now go and get on with your chores and leave me to work.'

I went out to Pa. 'What's the trouble, Pa? Who was he? You knowed him, didn't you?'

Pa was saddling the mare and he didn't answer right away. He pulled the cinch tight, putting his knee into the horse's side so she couldn't blow out and leave the saddle loose when he mounted. She was an old cunning.

'That was Major Morgan, son, and the column was part of Custer's old regiment, the Seventh.' He straightened up and put a hand on the saddle horn. 'Yes, I knew him several years back when he was at Laramie.'

'What's up, Pa? What's the troubles he talked of?'

'Ain't nothing to worry about, Ben. You just keep close to home and look after things. I'm going over to Captain Colby's with the Volunteers.'

And he mounted and rode off.

Pretty soon, Dave came trailing up the road. He had another dog now and he carried the old gun. Only I seen that the safety catch was mended. He was bursting with news and called out before he reached me: 'Major o' th' cavalry come. There's Injun trouble.'

'He was here before,' I said, 'and his name's Major Morgan.' That quieted him for a bit but when we'd settled in the barn and his dog and our Sam was sniffing for rats, he burst out again.

'It's the Sioux at Pine Ridge. They're dancin' th' ghost dance an' wearin' th' ghost shirts that Takawa told us about. The agent can't stop them so they've sent for the soldiers.'

'Pa's gone to Captain Colby's,' I said. 'Something about the Volunteers.'

Dave whistled and slipped the safety catch of the old gun back and forth. 'Then they must be expecting trouble. Wonder where 'Kawa is?'

But we couldn't find the Indian boy and presently Dave went back to help guard the house, so he said, and I went indoors and looked at the gun rack on the wall and went to ask Ma about the cartridges.

Well, that's about all of it, except what the soldiers done to the Indians. It wasn't till Christmas that it happened at a place called Wounded Knee Creek.

The snow come early that winter. We'd gone all through the hot summer praying for rain and then it came cold, sudden like. Afore you knowed it the leaves, which was burned brown anyway, fell off the trees and it was blowing down from the north and freezing. Snow begun to fall and I helped Pa stack up a wagon with straw and drive over to Takawa's so they could spread the straw in their tepee and keep warm. They had the animals in with them and Takawa looked cold and thin and Dave, who'd come with us, took him on one side and asked him what the ghost dancers were going to do now the soldiers had come but he didn't reply or say much at all.

Ma had put food in the wagon for the children. 'They got to eat, Injuns or no,' she had said and Pa had nodded. We drove back along the same tracks that the wagon had made through the snow coming out.

There'd been a lot of coming and going all fall and then one day, near Christmas, when the whole valley was white, Captain Colby and Mr Hannery and a lot of men come riding by and went off south after speaking to Pa. They were the Volunteers from all the ranches and homesteads round about, got together to protect the valley. They was all grim and quiet.

Pa stayed back to ride round the valley, calling on all the women in turn to see they was all right. Ma kept going out on to the porch all the time he was away, never minding the cold and watching the trail for him to come galloping back. And every time I slipped off from the house she would shout at me to come in.

Christmas was over when Captain Colby and the Volunteers came back. A mighty poor Christmas it was, with the men gone from the valley and no fun or visiting. We usually decorated the schoolhouse and had a play about the baby Jesus and the wise men but it wasn't like that this year I'm telling you about.

Kind of funny, really, when all the time the Indians was saying *their* Messiah had come.

When the men got back they was all excited and telling about fighting the Sioux and how the tribes were finished now once and for all and that there'd be no more ghost dances.

'You saw them first, Ben,' said Captain Colby, putting a hand on my head and smiling, though it was a hard sort of smile. 'You won't see ghosts in this valley any more.'

After that, no one took much notice of me, and Ma was too busy to head me off, what with getting them all things to eat and drink and so I just hung around and listened to the talk.

It seems the soldiers got all the dancers together for a council at Wounded Knee. Old Big Foot, and Kicking Bear and Yellow Bird and many others, though I didn't hear no mention of Sitting Bull. Mr Hannery said later that he guessed he was too cunning to come. They told the Indians that the ghost dances must stop, but, of course, the Sioux wouldn't agree.

Well, they argued for two days and the Indians kept coming and going and the soldiers cursed the cold and got impatient.

Then they rolled the gun to the top of a hill, looking down on all the Indians. It was a Hotchkiss gun, I heard someone say and that the battery commander would get a medal for his part in what had happened.

They said that the Indians had guns under their blankets and told them to give them up.

'But there were women and children there, too, weren't there?' I heard Pa ask.

The men argued a bit and some of them thought that there was. But they all agreed that they had guns hidden, even the squaws.

Finally, one old Indian got up and threw down his blanket and waved a gun at the soldiers who had been searching the tepees and the braves themselves, looking for rifles.

The men weren't at all clear about what happened then. They were someways off behind the soldiers and near some buildings. But anyway, that gun went off.

And Yellow Bird, this old chief, rose up and threw a handful of dirt in the air like it was a signal. And before the dust hit the ground some young braves leaped up and began shooting at the soldiers.

Then the Hotchkiss gun, that gun with wheels and the long barrel that we'd been so excited to see rolling through our valley, started to fire and send shells screaming down into the Indian camp. They burst among the tepees and knocked some of them down so that all the women and children ran away and hid in a ditch.

Some of the braves lined up and tried to protect them, but all the time the other Indians worked their rifles on the soldiers. Captain Colby said he'd never seen repeating rifles used so quickly or so smart.

Our men by the buildings couldn't do much on account of the soldiers and the Indians on the council square being all mixed up, fighting. But the team with the Hotchkiss gun fired at the Indian village all the time and I guess that's what won the battle in the end and why they're going to get a medal.

Only it don't seem right that they was firing at the squaws and their children, does it? Why, it might have been Takawa there.

After the battle the snow came and covered the ground and the dead so that when Mr Hannery and some men from our valley went back two-three days after there was nothing to see except just humps on the snow, hundreds of them. And the bodies were frozen stiff, so they said.

The men went among them turning them over to see if anyone was still alive and picking up ghost shirts for souvenirs.

Ma cried out when she heard that they found three babies all alive and an old woman. They took them back to the town where there was an Indian doctor to look after them.

But most of the Indians was killed. Old Yellow Bird and Big Foot, too, who had been with the ghost dancers when we first saw them that evening up near the creek.

I seen a picture of him in a newspaper; it's still around somewheres. He's sitting up in the snow, looking at the sky as if he expected Wovoka to come down with the snowflakes and save him. He's even got his arm stretched out. Only he's froze stiff with cold and he sat there for three days, with the wind blowing his black hair over his face, till they come and pulled him out and put him in a pit they dug.

Then the men who had done the burying all lined up and had *their* picture took standing round the big grave, full of dead ghost dancers and the painted shirts that didn't stop no bullets.

The Sioux rode for the last time at Wounded Knee and the dance they danced there was the dance of death.

I heard Mr Hannery tell Pa they got two dollars for every Indian they buried. I didn't know what to think about it all, at the end. Takawa went away into the hills and he didn't come back for nigh on three days.

I reckon he didn't want Dave and me to see him crying.

# Ghostly Experiences

### CHOSEN BY SUSAN DICKINSON

The remarkable revival of interest in ghost stories at the present time is curious, for ghost stories traditionally belong to that great age of story telling: the 19th century. And yet, despite the distractions of the television screen, ghost stories are much in demand particularly among the young. Here you will find examples of ghost stories ranging from R. L. Stevenson and J. S. LeFanu in the 19th century to the most contemporary of contemporary writers – Alan Garner and Joan Aiken.

Some of the stories are truly spine-chillers; some of the ghosts are gentle, some are not; but the collection should provide plenty of ghostly 'pleasure'.

'A splendid collection of supernatural adventures.'
*New Statesman*

'The stories in this collection have been chosen with discrimination and illustrated with a sure intuition.'
*Growing Point*

# The Black Cauldron

LLOYD ALEXANDER

Lloyd Alexander is one of America's most distinguished children's authors. He holds both the Newbery Medal and the National Book Award. *The Black Cauldron* is the second book in his Chronicles of Prydain, following *The Book of Three* which is also a Lion.

Once again Taran, the Assistant Pig-Keeper, and his ill-assorted band of followers are led into a world full of humour, enchantment and peril.

# The Book of Three

### LLOYD ALEXANDER

Lloyd Alexander is one of America's most distinguished children's authors. He holds both the Newbery Medal and the National Book Award. *The Book of Three*, a marvellous blend of mythology and Welsh legend, is the first title in his Chronicles of Prydain. It describes with rich humour and wisdom the adventures and misadventures of Taran, the Assistant Pig-Keeper, who longs to become a hero. His motley band of followers—hideous, hairy Gurgi, fiddler Flam, Doli the invisible dwarf, and the beautiful Princess Eilonwy—are as enchanting as his enemies are terrible.

The second book in the Chronicle, *The Black Cauldron*, is also a Lion.